When the Moon Fell

MJ Bowman

THE
OCEAN DEEP

When the Moon Fell by MJ Bowman

Copyright © 2022 MJ Bowman

All rights reserved. No portion of this book may be reproduced in any form without permission from the publisher, except as permitted by U.S. copyright law.

For permissions contact: makayla.jean@icloud.com

Cover by A. Bowman.

ISBN: 978-1-957674-05-6 (Paperback)

ISBN: 978-1-957674-21-6 (Digital)

Published by The Ocean Deep Publishing

13833 Dumfries Rd, Manassas, VA 20112

Printed in USA

*To my younger self,
who would have been terrified
to pick this book off the shelf.
It gets better, kid.
I promise.*

*To all those who watch the moon on restless nights,
missing someone.
May the stars guide you back together, one day.*

*To my family, blood or otherwise,
I love you to the moon and back <3*

I.

June twenty-sixth, 2020. 4:19 am.
There are three things you need to know.
My best friend disappeared five years ago, to the day.
The moon is only a few miles away from crashing into the Earth.
I can't leave her *here alone.*
"Stop the car!"

A clatter of boxes hit the front wall as the moving truck screeched to a stop. Kaiya Abbott and her father's chests slammed forward, only held back by their seatbelts. A chorus of glass shattering pierced the wall of the truck, quickly reaching the two pairs of ears. Mr. Abbott, red-faced with steam pouring out of his nostrils, furiously stared down his daughter from the driver's seat.

"Kaiya! What is the matter with you?" Mr. Abbott screamed, throwing his hands up from the steering wheel. The movement was so quick it seemed as if his crisp white button-down would rip a seam. He wracked his short, pristine black hair, waiting for an answer.

"I have to go. Explain later." The girl, tan considering it was only early Summer, brushed strands of dark hair from her eyes. Kaiya Abbott threw open the truck's passenger door without another glance towards her father and bounded out onto the metal steps. A gust of salty sea wind nearly knocked her off her feet as she entered the night.

She took off at a sprint as her black canvas shoes scraped against the gravel pavement, passing by a parked navy sedan, her mother climbing out and yelling after her. Kaiya followed the one-way road that twisted back into the thick treeline, the Maine seaboard stretching out into the opposite distance. Bright light caressed the landscape as if it were day while the nearby sound of crashing waves triumphed over the remaining nighttime calls of wildlife. Grey clouds enveloped the sky with only one thing to break their expansive coverage; the large face of the full moon.

"Kaiya! Get back here!" Mr. Abbott called out from his driver's side seat. He wracked his greying hair, looking back and forth from the dashboard, his wife, and his runaway daughter. His *only* daughter.

Kaiya kept running. The wind blew tears from her eyes, drying out her tear ducts and blurring her vision. Her lungs burned from the lack of oxygen as her legs stiffened, lactic acid building up in her calves and quads. Though ungiving, the familiar terrain was no match for Kaiya's five-year desire to find her lost friend. She sprinted on through the trails she knew all too well. Her feet pounded against the forest floor as the moving truck quickly disappeared from view. Not that she was looking back, anyways.

I need to go back to the cliff.

The moonlight filtered through the trees in a way that illuminated Kaiya's path. It was much darker under the coverage of the canopy, but that didn't seem to hinder Kaiya's will. She rushed onwards, jumping over rocks and pressing through the low-hanging branches. The trees reached out toward Kaiya with long, spindly fingers, aching to touch her warm skin. Vigorous winds pushed against her path, acting as a force of prevention to Kaiya. Though out of sight, covered by the thick glen of trees, the thundering crashes of ocean waves resounded in her ears.

I can't leave. Not yet.

In her haste, Kaiya ran straight into one of the branches.

Damnit!

Tears streamed down her face, turning pink with blood. A long, thin gash lined her cheekbone. The new dampness on her cheeks turned cold as the wind whipped through the narrowing treescape.

She kept sprinting.

Thick trees morphed into thinner saplings until Kaiya burst into a clearing between the forest and the sea. A few hundred yards away, the rocky edge of a cliff loomed over the tsunami-like tide. On the horizon, the Moon painted the shore with light. Not even a sliver of black sky could be seen past her enormous celestial face.

She glanced back towards the woods and beyond, the moving truck idled with all of her worldly possessions. Well, all except one.

"For five years, you've gotten closer and closer. First

the tides, then the animals, and gravity?" Kaiya started, aiming word encrusted daggers towards the sky. Her breaths came out in sharp gasps.

"You've ruined my life! You've taken *everything* from me!" She screamed, her voice raw from breathing in the whipped salty wind.

Below her feet, monstrous waves billowed up towards the top of the three-story cliff. The waves seemed to reach higher and higher into the sky, leaving tremendous troughs in their wake. Hot, brutal winds battered the coast, powered by the tides and earlier summer sun. The moon's increasingly close proximity to the blue planet caused a disturbance in the average weather patterns of Earth. Hurricane strength winds picked up beach chairs, umbrellas, and small pebbles, whipping them around like toddlers would whip their toys. The moon's gravity pulled heavily on the Earth's surface, tugging the sea and all else she could reach to join her among the stars.

Kaiya fell to her knees, the cliff's edge mere feet away. The sea peppered her body with tiny water droplets, momentarily softening the anger that teemed just beneath her skin.

The Moon's craters were larger than cumulonimbus clouds on the horizon. Every hill, depression, and mark on her surface could be seen with the naked eye. The fullness of her breadth couldn't be absorbed in a single glance, her pale light turning the night into day.

The grass stained Kaiya's fingertips as she raked for something concrete to hold on to. Blasts of wind whipped her black hair into mighty knots that disrupted her vision. As soon as tears hit her cheeks, they dried from the intensity of the wind.

"Is this some kind of sick joke to you? Five years to the day, huh?! You couldn't have picked some other time to crash into Earth?" She screamed into the face of the moon, so close she could almost touch her.

Of course, the moon didn't answer her pleas.

"To crash into me?"

Kaiya's parents searched for their daughter somewhere off in the surrounding forest. Their calls were mere whispers in the face of the pandemonium. The wind, waves, and sky all jockeyed for the auditory attention of those who had not already evacuated. It might have been a beautiful night if the world had not been swirling out of control.

Snippets of old videotapes flashed in Kaiya's head. Packed lunches, overalls, stickers, and white flowers rushed back into her senses. Her childhood had ended the night of June twenty-sixth, 2015, along with much of her will. Gone with the recession of the tide and disappeared like the light side of the Moon.

Five years of anger, blame, and resentment bubbled up to Kaiya's surface. Waves of fury towards Blair, the tide, the Moon, and herself spilled over the sides of her psyche.

"YOU TOOK OPAL FROM ME!" She screeched, her voice breaking and cracking under the pressure of her words.

The waves were deafening. Cyclones of wind uprooted entire plants and small trees, creating a vortex of weightless debris. Through the ensuing chaos, the Moon watched from her ever-closing position in the sky.

Gravity seemed to pull at every atom of Kaiya's

being, emotionally and physically. Her thoughts slipped from her mind into the very essence of the celestial body.

Let her go…

A voice, kind, familiar, and young, whispered into Kaiya's ear. Her breath caught up in her throat. From her pocket, Kaiya pulled out a thin glass case. Sandwiched between the glass squares was a pressed white flower, dried and yellowed at the edges from the passage of time.

"She's… gone." Kaiya breathed, barely a whimper. Her whole body seemed to go limp as the pressure evaporated from the atmosphere. The glass case slipped from her fingers, falling slowly until it landed a few feet away.

All at once, everything fell. The debris, the waves… And the moon.

II.

"Scientists from all over the world agree; the Moon will come into contact with Earth by June of this year, just under two months away." The reporter's voice whispered in through Kaiya's earbuds. The wire snaked down to the smartphone in her raincoat pocket. Her long, ebony hair was tied back in a low ponytail, just taut enough to keep it out of her face. Her eyes seemed to be set in a permanent squint, a vain attempt to keep the saltwater from turning her dark brown eyes bloodshot. People say that she looked like a feminine version of her father, which she consistently denied. She mainly wore dark colors, though it wouldn't be wise to call her "emo" unless one wished to sport a black eye to school the next day.

Black skinny jeans are comfortable, is all.

It was a groggy Sunday afternoon; the skies were grey and overcast. The Atlantic Ocean spray seemed colder than it should've been for an early May day. Kaiya kicked

11

small stones as she walked along the familiar shoreline of Niboiwi Bay.

"World officials have banded together to try and formulate solutions for this growing issue. Some politicians say that time is running out and scientists aren't working fast enough to solve the issue. In a statement from the NATO president...."

The end of days...

Kaiya's feet carried her into one of the abundant sea caves that adorned the Maine coastline. She had searched this cave so many times; her footprints scraped away imprints in the rock slabs.

She closed her eyes as her hand trailed along the damp stone wall. Her fingernails occasionally caught on moss peeking through the crevices. As she descended further into the cave, the sound of the crashing tides and cawing seagulls softened against the cave's rough limestone surface.

"In other news, it is expected that Governor Ronald Harvey, the incumbent governor of Maine, will include a plan to address the growing lunar concerns in his reelection campaign. Since the moon is the closest to Earth its ever been, there have been numerous changes to nature as we know it. Lunar cycles have grown longer, and the mating routines of local wildlife have been heavily disrupted. With all these natural changes, all eyes turn to Harvey to see what exactly the politician has in mind for his campaign—" The newscaster's voice crackled in and out of range as Kaiya plunged further into the darkness of the sea cave.

"Ugh. Every time." Kaiya grunted under her breath. One would think she'd be used to the occurrence by now. Sure, she had only started bringing her phone to the caves a few months ago, but Kaiya had always been well aware of the horrible service in the caves. Five years ago, Kaiya would run through these natural halls with only a walkie-talkie in her grasp. It never worked, but knowing that her best friend had a matching device was enough to keep the talkie on hand.

She pulled out her smartphone and clicked it on. Though she knew precisely what she'd see, the tiny icon in the corner confirmed her suspicion. No bars.

Kaiya looked up from her phone. Water droplets dripped quietly from the stalactite ceiling. The air grew cooler and dank as she descended down a familiar path. A tiny stream flowed down the limestone parallel to her trail, carrying salty seawater deep into the Earth. The water babbled, echoing whispers of sea tales against the ancient stone walls as it flowed.

As she continued down the worn trail, vague images resurfaced from the depths of her memory. Flashes of brightly colored clothes— rainbow stripes?— a packed lunch, and wildflowers danced through her mind's eye. Something was there, hidden between the grains of time.

I'm missing something.

Her head swam with questions from that night. Almost five years of grief had passed since Opal's disappearance. Opal was—

Is.

Opal *is* Kaiya's best friend since birth. Her matching puzzle piece, her quintessential counterpart. Her equal, yet also her balance. The sea and the sky, never one without the other. A connection so rare, so perfect, that the gods themselves must have pushed the two together.

Opal's parents, Mr. and Mrs. White, had processed their grief in a starkly different way than Kaiya. Once the police had deemed the search hopeless, all leads cold, the Whites had held a funeral for Opal. They buried an empty casket, denoted by a headstone for someone not yet passed. After the ceremony, the Whites had all of Opal's clothes and possessions donated, to aid in soothing the pain of losing their only daughter.

Everything was donated, except for one tiny object.

Kaiya pulled out a thin glass case. Sandwiched between the two square panes of glass was a white flower, dried out and yellowed at the edges from age. The gold-lined case was an antique from Kaiya's mother, Mrs. Margaret Abbot. The flower, however, was the only thing Opal had left behind before she disappeared.

She thumbed over the glass, checking for scratches or damage. Kaiya pulled the edge of her sleeve down and used it to smooth out the thumbprints. She lifted the glass up to her eye and looked through the glass, past the flower, to see the cave. The yellowed flower, its species not yet identified, was one of the only things Kaiya had left from that June day all those years ago. When Kaiya had arrived at the hospital after Opal's disappearance, soaked and coughing up water, she held a death grip on the handle of a tan wicker basket. The police took almost everything inside the basket as evidence; the walkie-talkies, plastic sandwich bags, and wooden cutlery—except for a lone, pale, fragile blossom. Part of one of its petals was torn, but Kaiya didn't care. It was the one thing of Opal's she was allowed to keep from that day.

There must be something else here. Even after all this time…

Kaiya sighed and put the memento back into her jacket pocket. She walked further down into the cave, almost reaching her destination. Her feet could've carried her the rest of the way if her eyes had been closed.

Her fingers trailed along the damp limestone. The walls were a balance of slimy stone and fuzzy moss. The stray beams of light thinned as Kaiya Abbot descended the natural hallway. Time seemed to reverse, slowly creeping back through the years until 2020 morphed back into June twenty-sixth, 2015. The air grew damp, invading Kaiya's lungs as the faint scent of honey drifted down the hallway adjacent to Kaiya as she walked. Possibly it was just the feeling of descending deeper into the cave, but Kaiya felt herself shrink, growing smaller, receding into herself as she slowly became thirteen again.

Just as the darkness seemed to encapture Kaiya, the cave opened up into a grand atrium. Lines from sediment deposits ringed around the high ceiling, denoting the water level from previous annual cycles. The cave walls in this space were much smoother than the last channel Kaiya had passed through. A skylight pierced through the atrium's ceiling, opening up to the great blue sky above and letting in a few shining rays of sunlight.

Beside the pathway, the small stream trickled into a delicate tidal pool. The pool was simple and beautiful, seeming to be only a few feet deep. However, high tide would flood the turquoise waters and envelope the sea caves in saltwater.

And all those caught inside.

Kaiya winced, only able to remember an infinite,

cold darkness pierced by a blinding light.

And then she was gone. Opal...

My *Opal*.

Kaiya pushed her thoughts away.

There has to be a clue here somewhere—something I've missed.

She closed her eyes, bringing her old memories to the surface of her mind's eye. The atrium seemed brighter in her memory, less cold and dreary.

Kaiya opened her eyes and walked through the time capsule.

Opal set up the picnic blanket here...

She sat down on a flat boulder that overlooked the pool. The entrance to the atrium and its path snaked to the right of the glimmering water—the only exit.

Kaiya surveyed the odd architecture the sea had carved into the stone. It was easy to understand why the best friends had often visited these caves. When the sun shone just right, the walls seemed to cast rainbows over the pool. Gentle, trickling water provided the perfect ambiance for a quiet afternoon together, Kaiya's head resting in Opal's lap as she rambled on about the stars.

She shut her eyes, and the mirage disappeared. The backs of her hands rubbed at her eyelids in a vain attempt to stall the tears. When she looked up again, the light took on a sharper slant, denoting the onset of dusk. Upon closer examination, the rays of sunlight that angled through the skylight high above her seemed to take on a bright cerulean hue.

Huh...?

"Kaiya? Are you down there?" Mrs. Abbott called

out from atop the skylight that opened up to the surface of a cliff. Only a thin barricade of wire warned the passing people of the vertical passageway into the cave below. Kaiya couldn't see her mom through the opening but knew she was leaning over the wire and pointing, what Kaiya assumed, was a portable blue spotlight down into the abyss. Mrs. Abbott was constantly working on new photographic projects, most of them dealing with color and the refraction of light. The blue spotlight was most likely a new toy that kept her mom holed up in her studio for hours on end.

It was a wonder that she had even interrupted her work to find Kaiya.

"Yeah, Mom. I'm here. I told you I was going for a walk, just like I always do on the weekends. What's wrong?" Kaiya raised her voice so it would carry all the way to the top of the cliff, where her mother, no doubt, was anxiously awaiting her response.

"You said you would be home before high tide at dusk. I have a huge new piece that I'm doing, and I can't have you out wandering the coast or, God-forbid…" Mrs. Abbott paused, tentative. "Well, *drowning* while I'm working on it."

Home? I'm not even sure if that is my home anymore. Not without Opal there.

"Fine. I'll be right up."

Kaiya glanced around the cave once more, searching for something. For what, she didn't quite know. She sighed. Nothing quite jumped out at her, screaming, "Look at me! Look at me! I'm a clue!" Defeated, Kaiya dragged her feet back to the entrance of the rocky room.

She reached out and touched the natural doorway

with her fingertips, slick and cold.

I'll be back soon. Just wait for me, okay, Opal?

Kaiya's image proceeded into the darkness on her way back 'home.'

III.

Time tends to cast a faint shadow over the fine details of memories, especially traumatic ones that fight to be forgotten. Every day since June twenty-sixth, 2015, perpetually and incessantly, Kaiya would turn to the one thing she knew could concretely aid her recollection of that fateful date.

Video Home System tapes.

Though technology has long since surpassed the need for film-based videography, the large, chunky VHS camcorders served as a reminder of a simpler time without unlimited access to infinite information and endless sociocultural complications. When Kaiya was behind the camcorder, everything was alright.

At least, for the most part.

After a predominantly silent dinner, then proceeded with cleaning up the dinner table and kitchen *and* taking Blaine out for her nightly walk, Kaiya was able to finally sit

19

down and enjoy her evening. Well, if you can call reliving the disappearance of her best friend "enjoyment," anyhow.

She tended to spend a good chunk of her time in the darkness of the basement, laying on the hot-pink bean bag chair, curled up with a fuzzy lilac blanket that was just a smidge too small for her. Along the walls were photographs of the Abbott family, immediate and extended. Most of the photos were of Kaiya as a toddler, surrounded by smiling adults and other small children. The most recent picture was one of Kaiya, eleven or twelve, and her parents posing as a historical family in one of those antique style booths that frequent fairs and carnivals. The ones where mothers pull their children and husbands through the saloon-style doors and dress up in elaborate gowns and tuxedos. Extraneous preparation for a two-second photograph of the family. No smiles. Someone always blinks. This photograph, in its golden embossed frame, housed a thick layer of dust, considering Mrs. Abbott was quite the neat freak. For a modern house, the basement wasn't as large as one would think it would be. The Abbott home mainly dealt with "would be" and "should be," nothing concrete. Nothing absolute.

Yet, the basement is the only place on the Abbott property, other than the greenhouse, that Kaiya felt she truly was real, sentient. Elsewhere, she felt dimmed. A shadow of herself that only floated over the hardwood. Merely an afterimage of who she could have been. Who she *should* have been.

Regardless of "could" and "should," what *was* was the VHS camcorder. The comically colossal camera, black with silver accents, sat adjacent to the wooden hutch that housed the large, flat-screen TV. A juxtaposition of technology, old and new, tended to give Kaiya a spark of joy. Not much, but enough to aid her strength to continue her mission.

She popped out the VHS tape from within the camcorder. Deftly, she slid the VHS into the VHS player that perched on a dusty shelf within the hutch. The VHS player was one of the few things in the Abbott house that definitely showed its age. Its corners were dented, the paint having worn off years prior. The heat vents on the sides wheezed and puffed out dust in a struggled attempt to keep the machinery cool— like an old smoker sitting alone in a retirement home, simply waiting for his timer to be up.

A little light turned on, and the TV buzzed to life.

If she were better at art, which she wished she was, Kaiya would have been able to draw a perfect recreation of every frame of this tape. She'd watched and rewatched and rewatched the video again and again and again—hopelessly searching for a clue—some sort of hint as to what *actually* happened that summer night.

Opal thought I was a good artist...

Light peeked in from the edges of the frame. Orange numbers in the bottom right corner of the screen read out the date of the tape: 06/26/15. The sound was muffled, as if listening through a wool sweater.

The dark screen, now cleaned so that the lens was crystal clear, opened up to a hardwood floor. Not the woodwork of the Abbott house; no, these floor panels were much lighter in color. More worn in. Lived in without the constant pressure to be kept clean.

These were the floors of the White house. Opal

White's house that is.

Kaiya's hands came into view of the screen, her fingers much smaller than they were now, painted pink, orange, and white, chipped and careless. Kaiya's thirteen-year-old self waved her hand in front of the lens.

"And we're live! C'mon, Opal. Let's go ask your parents if we can head down to the caves today. My Mom says that it should be a Supermoon tonight, whatever that is," Young Kaiya giggled, " and I'd love to see it with you!" Her younger self's voice burst through the speakers. High pitched, not quite as resentful. Jubilant.

Those were the days, huh.

The camcorder looked up from the hardwood, and there she was.

Opal White.

Only freshly thirteen at the time of the recording, her bright, blue eyes shone like sunlight off the sea's water. Dark freckles peppered the surface of her light skin, like an undeveloped negative of the night sky. Her hair fell just past her shoulders like cascades of bright blonde silk— waving slightly, going with the flow of the bends. She always wore overalls, the same pair with an embroidered flower on the front pocket. Today, she wore a short sleeve rainbow-striped shirt underneath her denim overalls. Opal was short for her age, a whole four foot eleven and five-eighths, but it never dampened her spirit. Her light-up Sketchers illuminated her way through the adversity, past the bullies. It was as if Opal couldn't even see those who held ill will towards her. Blinders shielded her eyes from the negativity that dominated middle school. She had—

Has.

She *has* round cheeks that lift up whenever she smiles, and she smiles quite frequently. Opal wore glittery silver eyeshadow just in the corners of her eyes. "It attracts boys," she would always say with a wink, though she never talked about boys other than in tandem with the eyeshadow.

What I would give to see her wink again.

"Really! A Supermoon! Let's go!" Opal reached past the camera's view, grabbing Kaiya's hand and leading her through the house. The camera jostled around, fading in from the darkness of Kaiya's shirt to the blurred birch floor panels and emerald green walls. The Whites had a thing for green.

The sound of the two girls running came to a halting stop, the camera still pointing downwards towards their feet. Kaiya was wearing plain, black ankle socks while Opal wore two mismatched socks; one had a cartoon fox, and the other had a camel with a paintbrush.

Yes. A camel with a paintbrush.

From off-screen, there was a knock. Presumably by Opal on Mr. White's office door, which he usually kept open. The camera tilted up ever so slightly to show that the door was, in fact, ajar, and Opal was simply knocking out of courtesy. Inside the office, Mr. White sat behind a Victorian-style desk. He looked up from his laptop, an odd object to rest on such an antique, and ushered the two girls inside with a wave of his hand. Mr. White was a jovial man, a biology teacher at the local high school. When he wasn't working on lesson plans, he played chess or Hearts with his wife and daughter. His hair was a chestnut brown, curled at the ends, and lay just below the edge of his graying eyebrows. The lines that creased the corners of his turquoise eyes were not from age, even though he was a few years younger than Kaiya's parents, but from smiling.

Still, the camcorder pointed towards the ground. Off the screen, Mr. White's soothing baritone voice echoed off of the office walls.

"What's up, Arty Opal and Classy Kaiya? Do you guys need more juice-" Mr. White said, chuckling, and the camera shook a little.

"C'mon, Dad! We're thirteen, not six!" Opal said, giggling. Even when her dad poked fun at Opal's childish charm, she couldn't stay mad at him for long.

"Oh, right, right. I forgot that your birthday was only a few days ago, Opal." Mr. White sighed.

Mr. White had tucked a piece of hair from Opal's face. I remember him looking down and smiling at Opal. The last time he would see her for a while…

"Hey, Daddy, do you mind if Kaiya and I go down to the caves to watch the Supermoon tonight? We'll be back before it gets too late!" Opal asked, her voice many octaves higher than her dad's.

Mr. White considered it for a moment. The camcorder angled towards Mr. White's sandals, his main shoe choice for the summertime.

"Oh, what the heck! It's not like you two don't go there all the time, anyways. Just be back before ten, okay?"

The two girls squealed, "Yay!"

Opal's mismatched socks were standing on Mr. White's sandals, the two in a tight embrace. Mr. White then leaned over and gave Kaiya a quick hug.

"Now, before you leave, I would like you to say goodbye to your mom. She's out back in the garden." Mr.

White remarked, shooing the girls towards the glass door that led outside.

The camera angle jostled once more as the two pre-teens skidded over to the sliding back door, which led to the White garden. It was a massive space, spanning the whole width of the house and receding down a slight hill, over which the ocean came to light. There were rows upon rows of flowerbeds: red tulips, orange peonies, and yellow sunflowers, all atop a base of green stems, leaves, and vines. There were bluebells, irises, hyacinths, and daisies, some hanging from twine and others climbing up intricate metal trellises. So much life, so much color, it was almost blinding. Indeed, it was as if Mrs. White had lowered a rainbow-colored lens over the eyes of all who gazed at her garden.

The camera panned up as young Kaiya walked out the glass door, sliding it shut behind her. Mrs. White stooped over one of her many garden beds, encased in carved wooden pots. The shining summer sun illuminated her blonde hair, the same shade as Opal's, which was tied back with a baby blue ribbon in a low bun. A wide-brimmed straw hat shaded Mrs. White's face, angular, with sharper cheekbones than her daughter. Nonetheless, Mrs. White's face burst into a wide, toothy grin at the sight of her daughter and her best friend, an honorary White daughter. She stood up and brushed the dirt off of her blue jean capris, and discarded the brown gardening gloves she had been wearing. Mrs. White opened her arms up to the two children, a welcoming gesture that fit the Garden of Eden atmosphere.

"C'mere girls! Give Mama White a hug!"

Mama White... she hardly ever calls herself that anymore.

"Hi, Mama! Kaiya n' I are heading down to the caves to watch the Supermoon. Daddy said to come visit you first before we left." Opal said, slightly muffled since she talked right into Mrs. White's coveralls.

The camera angle was faced down again, most likely because young Kaiya was too busy watching Opal and her mom embrace.

Mrs. White always gave the best hugs.

"You too, Kaiya! Bring it in!" Mrs. White's cheerful soprano-like voice sang through the audio of the VHS player, a message through time. With that statement, the camera went dark as young Kaiya, Opal, and Mrs. White embraced in a group hug.

The trio disbanded as the hug came to an end.

"Oh! You should make it into a picnic! A little girl's date, yeah? I'll go grab some snacks to bring with you on your little adventure!" Mrs. White wiped her hands on the front of her coveralls, turned on the heels of her baby blue flats, and headed back inside the house.

The frame stuttered for a minute and then resumed, the camera now looking at the inside of the White's kitchen.

Mrs. White handed Opal a tan wicker basket, the ones with flaps on top that were always in the movies.

"Well, you two be safe down there. I want you back before the tide rolls in, okay? I love you two so much. Now, go have fun!" Mrs. White ushered the two girls out in a similar fashion to Mr. White, a gesture probably born from the many years they spent together.

"Thanks, Mama!" Opal called back.

How I wished that I could call her Mama, too.

Young Kaiya and Opal rushed out the glass door that led to White Garden, running through the rows of flower beds and viney trellises. The bright spring sun was three-quarters of the way through her journey across the sky. On the opposing end of the horizon, the moon's shadow watched over the Maine coastline, silently waiting for her turn to rule the heavens.

The next few minutes of the video were mostly silent, interrupted by the occasional "ope!" as one of the girls would stumble and catch her balance. Opal and young Kaiya carefully descended the steep trail that led from White Garden down to Niboiwi Beach. It was a similar path to the trail that led up to the Abbott house. However, this trail was quite a bit longer since the White house sat at a higher elevation than the Abbott house. Nonetheless, the longer route was just as beautiful as the garden that sat atop it. Flower seeds that drifted down the slope from the White Garden had nestled themselves between the sharp slabs of stone that rested alongside the gravel trail and bloomed into a trail of honeysuckles. No longer was the trail grey, sandy, and yellowed with age. Now, it looked as if the Goddess of spring, Persephone, had walked down the hill towards the beach, growing flowers in her wake.

Kaiya blinked a few times, realizing she had kept her eyes open for most of the video. A few tears flowed down her cheeks, not solely from her dry eyes. She rubbed her eyelids with the back of her hands, bright colors bursting like fireworks against her dark eyelids from the pressure. When Kaiya opened her eyes again, she pulled out her smartphone from her pocket to look at the time.

11:17 pm.

Ugh. I have school tomorrow.

Kaiya would still finish analyzing the video, though. It's not like there was much for her to pay attention to at school, anyways. She only needed one credit to graduate, so all of her other classes were simply for fun. Pottery. Photography. Poetry. Kaiya could have—should have—graduated early. There was no sense in her staying to finish her senior year at Atlantic High School. Only one thing held Kaiya back from moving on.

Opal.

"ACK! The camcorder!" Young Kaiya yelped from the speakers, quickly jostling Kaiya from her school-driven trance. The flat-screen TV monitor went black, only the blocky orange digits of the date showing that the TV wasn't off completely.

"Oh no! Is your mom's camera okay?" Opal cried out, garbled with a hint of static.

Young Kaiya lifted the camera from the ground. The screen had a thin crack on its surface, and the audio wasn't of the same quality as before. Other than those minor issues, the camcorder seemed to be okay.

"Yeah, I think it's fine. I just slipped on some of the rocks, and I dropped the camera. My mom shouldn't care much, anyways. She hasn't used this camera in years." Young Kaiya remarked, flipping the camera around to access the damage.

No matter how many times Kaiya watched this video, it always came as a slight shock to see her younger self. Her dark brown eyes still had a sense of light to them, and her eyebrows weren't set in a permanent furrow. Bits of black hair would fall out of her double braids, courtesy of

Opal's deft fingers, and would frame her face like a childish digital filter. She wore a neon pink shirt with a sequined unicorn across the front. Sure, she was thirteen and a full-fledged middle schooler. But, around Opal, Kaiya could wear the things she wanted to, the things that made her happy to wear. It didn't matter what anyone else said; it only mattered that she and Opal were completely genuine with each other. True and open.

During this time, Kaiya would wear navy glitter in the corners of her eyes.

"Dark blue, like the ocean. I know how much you love the ocean, Kaiya." Opal said once at a sleepover where the two had snuck into Mrs. Abbott's vanity, ruffling through the many shades of eyeshadow and blush the photographer kept on hand. Opal had fallen asleep soon after the makeover; the eyeshadow smeared across her lids and brow. She always was such a heavy sleeper.

I haven't worn eyeshadow since then.

The image of her younger self left as soon as she came, the camera now facing Opal, the dark Atlantic Ocean receding out to the far reaches of the horizon behind her. Young Kaiya had stuck her tongue out from behind the camera, causing Opal to laugh, a full laugh, not one held back for fear of embarrassment. That was Opal, unapologetically her. In this frame, the camera could more closely see the tiny acne spots that peppered her cheeks, forehead, and nose. Red freckles, she would call them—a sign of blossoming growth, like a flower just starting to open. A few straggling spots of acne dotted her neck. The rainbow-striped shirt she wore had a circular hem, just barely showing her collarbones, sharp and delicate, not yet caressed by the hands of time.

During the closeup, one thing always caught Kaiya's attention. For a split second, Opal's figure, the sea, and the sky would line up in perfect unison. Opal's eyes mirror the sky; blue, vast, and curious. The denim edges of her overalls would melt into the distant water of the sea, ebbing and flowing with Opal's movement. Her hair, a wavy blonde mirage of strands, would slip seamlessly into the sandy beach. All at once, it seemed as if Opal was Kaiya's world. Her vision; all that she could see.

"C'mon, Kay! This basket is getting heavy!" Opal said, holding back her giggles and turning away from the camera.

Kaiya sighed at the memory of her formerly used nickname. She shook her head and pulled a few stray strands of hair away that had fallen into her face—a futile attempt to ground herself.

She used to call me that all the time...

The camera now framed greyish rocky slabs instead of the former sandy, flowered pathway. Each step the girls took sent an audible, high-pitched squeak out of the speakers. When young Kaiya dropped the camera, she must have damaged the audio recorder as well as the glass lens. The new terrain the girls were traversing was more damp and slippery than the previous sandy trail had been. The exasperated squeaking persisted throughout the rest of the recording, much to Kaiya's dismay.

The screen stuttered again, the scene shifting from the dark entrance to the cave to a much brighter location.

There's so much missing...

Young Kaiya panned the camera up from her feet,

capturing the atrium with the camera's barrel. Opal was bent over, turned away from the camera as she set down the wicker basket on a flat rock, roughly hip height, that the two usually sat on when they visited the atrium. Bright light filtered in through the skylight, casting rainbows over the quiet babbling brook that flowed parallel to the atrium's entrance. The water collected in a seemingly shallow pool, crystal clear until the darkness of depth obscured the pool's bottom. Above the small pond, an extended network of green vines canvassed the stone wall. Full, white flowers bloomed along the vines, adding a heavenly liveliness to the atrium. The remaining cave walls shimmered, moist from condensation, as if millions of tiny crystals were embedded between the sedimentary lines. Opal stood back up and turned on her tip-toes, her hair whipping around like a silk curtain, and faced young Kaiya and the camera.

"Well, are you going to just stand in the doorway all day? Or are you going to help me set up this picnic!" Opal threw her hands up and out from her sides, exasperated. A red and white checkered blanket was hanging out of the picnic basket, waiting to be smoothed out. Opal tilted her head to one side and raised an eyebrow. Her hands finally found a comfortable place to rest: on her hips, slightly above the pockets of her overalls, just barely cinching in her waist.

"I, uh, duh! Sorry." Young Kaiya stuttered, running over to her best friend, obviously caught in her moment of staring. She set the camcorder down on the flat slab, positioning it so it faced the two girls as they examined the contents of the wicker basket. Behind them, just out of sight of the camera, was the entrance to the atrium and the pool that swirled adjacent to it.

"OH! EM! GEE!" Opal squealed, looking at something in the basket.

"What is it?" Young Kaiya said, startled, as she leaned over Opal's shoulder, resting her chin on Opal's overalls' strap to look in the basket.

"My mom packed us honeysuckles! She must have just harvested them. Here," Opal pulled out a honeysuckle, white and fragile, with a yellow, honey-covered stem sprouting from the center of the petals, and handed it to Kaiya.

"Aww, yay! We'll eat them at the same time, 'kay?" Young Kaiya said, looking at Opal, holding her flower out towards her best friend as if to toast the sweet treats.

"That sounds good! Ready? Three, two, one!" Opal said, delight creasing the corners of her eyes. The two best friends pulled the stems out from the middle of the flower. The nectar, bright yellow and saccharine, coated the thin strands that remained on the stem. Opal and Kaiya raised the stems up to their lips and popped the sugary ends onto their tongues. The two girls closed their eyes, savoring the sweet taste of the honeysuckle.

Young Kaiya was the first one to open her eyes again. She pulled the stem out from her mouth, having tasted all the nectar the flower had to offer. Opal still had her eyes closed, leaning back on her arms that rested on the flat stone. The honeysuckle's stem still poked out from between her lips, like a farmer with straw. One stray curl laid across Opal's brow, a perfect strand but just slightly blocking out one of Opal's eyes. Light streamed in from the skylight, at a steeper angle now, and cast a golden glow over Opal's body. The sedimentary rings around the atrium seemed to be placed in such a way that a halo rested atop her head. Angelic.

Young Kaiya moved her hand towards Opal, attempting to move the strand of hair from her face. To gently tuck it behind her ear, only barely grazing Opal's skin.

"Mmm, I could eat a whole tub of these!" Opal said, opening her eyes and sitting back up again. Young Kaiya quickly took her hand away, playing it off by tucking her own hair behind her ear.

"Yup! They're just so sweet. It's addicting." Young Kaiya managed to look Opal in the eyes, then quickly turned away.

Oi vey. I don't think I've ever seen a more socially awkward thirteen-year-old, especially around her best friend. I don't remember acting like that.

Then, the tape clicked off. Frozen on the image of Kaiya looking towards the ground, Opal's head tilted towards her best friend like a curious dog, ears pricked up.

That's the last thing that I can remember. The last time I ever saw her...

In her pocket, her phone buzzed, sending a momentary jolt through her body. It was easy to forget that the world still turned while Kaiya was remembering Opal.

Kaiya pulled out her phone and clicked it on. The time at the top of her screen drew her attention more than the flood of message notifications: 12:09 am.

"Kaiya? Kaiya, are you still up? There's something you need to see." Mrs. Abbott's voice called down the staircase from the living room. Her voice shook slightly as she spoke, like keys that rattled ever so slightly against each other in a denim pocket.

"What is it? I just want to sleep, Mother. C'mon." Kaiya groaned, flopping backwards into the bean bag.

"It's from the Governor." Mrs. Abbott responded, a bit quieter.

"So? Since when do you care what the Governor says?"

Mr. Abbott cleared his voice, joining his wife at the top of the staircase.

Like a zombie rising up from the ground, Kaiya lifted her fatigued limbs from the safety of the bean bag. She slugged over to the stairway so she could look directly at her parents. When Mr. Abbott cleared his voice, you knew it was serious.

Kaiya leaned against the wooden banister at the base of the carpeted staircase. Above, both of her parents stood cross-armed, with Mrs. Abbott standing slightly behind husband. Mr. Abbott cleared his throat. Again.

Not a good sign.

"Well, *Governor* Harvey just issued an evacuation order for the entire coast of Maine."

IV.

Kaiya stood in disbelief at the bottom of the basement stairs and looked up at her parents, tall, looming concrete statues with eyes of cold stone.

Evacuate…? As in, leave?

"Come upstairs. Now." Mr. Abbott said as he turned on his heel back towards the living room, not wasting a moment. Mrs. Abbott lingered at the top of the stairs, paint splattered on her work jeans and grey tee shirt.

No, no, no, no, no, NO. We can't leave now. Not when I'm so close.

Kaiya locked eyes with her mother, and, for a brief second, the two women understood one another. A shot of unknown, dosed in fear, coursed through them. Kaiya eventually broke eye contact and looked back down towards the gray carpet runner that cushioned the dark wooden stairs. With her right hand, she guided herself up the staircase, feeling every dent in the wooden rail under her fingertips as she rose from the darkness of the basement.

"I—" Kaiya started as she reached the landing at the top of the stairs.

"Shh. Go." Mrs. Abbott interrupted, her skin ghostly pale, a worn trampoline piled with snow so taut it could snap at any moment.

With her head down, Kaiya drifted towards the love seat, its red velvet surface bathed in the bluish light of the television.

"Today, May tenth, 2020, started out as a normal day for most citizens of the great state of Maine," A cheery reporter commented.

I swear, all reporters have the same voice.

Kaiya finally looked up from the ground and locked eyes with a blonde-haired woman, a badge hung haphazardly from a neon lanyard around her neck.

"Within the past hour," the reporter continued, "Governor Ronald Harvey changed the lives of many Maine citizens, declaring that those who live within ten miles of the Atlantic Coast must evacuate their homes by the end of this June, including our town of Acadia. In his emergency press meeting just a few moments ago, Governor Harvey stated…"

On the flatscreen, the image of the reporter shifted to the silhouette of a balding man standing behind a podium. The Maine state flag hung behind his broad shoulders and even broader stomach.

"As you all are most certainly aware, the issue of the moon has grown to an unproportionate size. I don't make this decision lightly, but under the guidance of my elite staff of scientists, I am now issuing Evacuation

Order number one hundred and twelve, which will go into effect immediately. By June twenty-ninth, all persons living within ten miles of the Atlantic or any subsequent bodies must evacuate inland. Under closer speculation, this issue has since been elevated from an event of concern to a state of clear emergency. There will be some financial compensation for persons affected by the evacuation mandate. That is all." Governor Harvey nodded toward the huge crowd of reporters, waved his hand, and left the podium. His entourage of security pushed through the thick congregation of newscasters, all shouting for some sort of elaboration from the governor. Despite their yelling, the Governor walked calmly out of the frame.

"Wow, Chuck. Can you believe that? Looks like life is about to flip upside down for a good chunk of the state! Guess I'll have to start packing my bags, right?" The reporter's blonde hair bounced around as she laughed.

This woman can't be real. This can't be real. An evacuation?

"Alrighty then, Chuck? What does our weather look like for the week?" The ditsy reporter said. The screen shifted, yet again, to an older man, presumably Chuck, in front of a large weather map.

Onto the next story. As if nothing had even happened. As if the world around Kaiya wasn't crumbling to pieces, slipping through her fingers like sand swept in the tide.

Just another regular Sunday evening.
This isn't happening.
Kaiya crumpled to the floor, her body turning to jelly. Green and blue lights from the flatscreen cast hallucinogenic shadows across her temples, shielding her

eyes from comprehending the gravity of the situation.

Ha. Gravity.

You know, because of the moon.

Blaine scampered over to where Kaiya knelt, her eyes still glued to the flatscreen. Chuck, the weatherman, was going on and on about some windstorm caused by air off the sea. The world around Kaiya spun, the cyclone officially in her living room, the ocean flowing from her eyes in stormy tears. Blaine was just a blur of white in the scattering colors that streaked Kaiya's vision.

"Get up. It's not like the world is ending. We will stay here until you've finished out your tenure at Atlantic High, and then we are leaving. We'll use one of my real estate investments more inland." Mr. Abbott said, barked? His voice pierced through the whirlwind of Kaiya's senses, overstimulated and hazy.

"What... Leave? No, it's just for a few weeks, right? Until they can figure out how to stop the moon?" Kaiya blinked, her hands finding comfort in Blaine's soft fur, an anchor in the tumultuous sea.

"Did you not hear Harvey?!" Mrs. Abbott screamed, stepping out from Mr. Abbott's shadow. "We're done! Gone! No more Abbott Hill or Niboiwi Bay for us!" She cackled, her eyebrows raised, arms thrown out to the sides. Her fingers, curled but not in fists, shook as if an earthquake was rocking her very foundation.

"Margaret. Calm yourself." Mr. Abbott sneered through his teeth, only looking at his wife through the peripheral of his vision. Mrs. Abbott's mouth fell into a thin line, quivering but not enough for her husband to seem to notice.

"As for you," Mr. Abbott turned slightly to look down at his daughter. "Get up. There's no need to throw a temper tantrum. It's not like you have anyone left here to miss when we leave."

He did not just say that.

Hot tears streaked Kaiya's flushed cheeks. No one left to miss, huh?

"You—" Kaiya seethed through her pursed lips.

"Go to your room! *NOW*." Mr. Abbott snapped, his stern hand pointing up the staircase. Blaine jumped back at the sudden outburst of noise, hiding behind Kaiya's crisscrossed form.

Kaiya sniffed, trying to hold back more tears. She needed to look strong, fierce, unbothered. She wouldn't, couldn't, let her father win. Not this time. Using her hands as braces, Kaiya pushed herself up from the ground.

Her eyes stared straight into Mr. Abbott's, her head only slightly inclined to look at him. Her lips were a tight line, her cheeks gleaming with salty tears. Her eyes, however, burned with fire behind her dark irises.

No one breathed.

Mr. Abbott stared her down, a muscle twitching in his forehead. Neither moved.

They must have stood there for hours, considering the intensity of their stares. Instead, Blaine came between the father and daughter, a fluffy barrier. Kaiya broke eye contact with Mr. Abbott to meet Blaine's deep blue eyes.

I'm so sorry, baby.

"C'mon, Blaine. Let's go to bed." Kaiya murmured, turning on her heel towards the staircase. Mrs. Abbott moved as if to reach out towards her but thought better of it, her hands retreating back to her sides. From her peripheral vision, as she shuffled across the living room, Kaiya could see Mr. Abbott straighten out his suit jacket and walk away into his office.

Unbothered.

Kaiya sulked up the stairs, Blaine hugging her heels as she ascended the brown diamond-patterned carpet runner. She padded over to her bedroom door and opened it. Light flooded into her eyes where the darkness of night should have been, causing her to shut her eyes.

Jeez, that's bright. Did someone install a lighthouse while I was gone?

Kaiya slowly opened her eyelids to adjust to the bright light, trying to find the source. Normally, the bay window next to Kaiya's bed faced the beach. On a night like this, she would have been able to see the stars that speckled the sky, tracing their constellations with her mind's eye.

Now, however, there wasn't a star in sight.

Her fullness enveloped at least half of the horizon. She shone twice as bright as the poets described and pulled at the ocean with ferocity, the waves meeting the sky just to graze her surface. Never touching, but always a balance of pushing and pulling.

Moon rays streaked across the carpet flooring of Kaiya's room. In her window was a suncatcher, its colors dulled from age. Now, the suncatcher refracted rainbows across Kaiya's ceiling. The bright colors of the refracted moonlight drew her in like fish to a lure.

It's never done that before. Hell, I can't even remember who gave me that suncatcher in the first place.

Kaiya touched the glass suncatcher for a moment, the metal edge cold against her fingers. She closed her eyes, reaching back into her memories for the gift giver's name. A fruitless search, especially after her concussion. Kaiya shrugged, dropping her hand from the suncatcher, and turned towards her bed.

Even though the full moon's light blazed her room into day, Kaiya collapsed onto her bed and slept, muscles finally relaxing under the moon's opalescent gaze.

V.

Condensation formed on the cool glass of the Biology classroom windows that looked out over Niboiwi Bay. A slight breeze off the surface of the bay drifted through the trees outside of Atlantic High School.

Kaiya walked in through the battered wooden doorway of Advanced Biology and sulked to her desk, a routine that was practically muscle memory by now. Second row, closest to the windows. Close enough that she could hear her homeroom teacher but far enough away that she could blend in with her peers.

She never lifted her eyes up from her feet, tracing their steps on the square tiles. The floors were off-white, speckled with black dots. Whether or not they were scuff marks from the millions of students who trampled the floor or not was a mystery. Even the oldest teachers here couldn't remember what the original floor looked like. Not that it mattered, anyhow. It's not like there was much use in renovating the floors of a small-town Maine high school when the moon was about to crash into Earth.

Considering we're closest to Niboiwi Bay, you would think the school would be named after the bay instead of the Atlantic Ocean. Oh, well. Guess we'll never know.

Kaiya gazed out across the bay, its horizon receding into the sky, both a shade of dark blue. The blackness of morning hadn't entirely disappeared, creating an image of an infinite ocean that stretched up into the atmosphere. The moon hung over the towering Ash trees, stoic guardians of the school. She was just a sliver, a crescent of her whole but nonetheless impressive in her sights. Dim rays of moonlight illuminated the surrounding forest. Though she cast the spotlight, all eyes were on her celestial radiance. The western sky was overflowing with her presence, white and pearly. The night sky was reduced to the Eastern horizon, along the ocean's surface, in which only a few stars could be seen.

"It's gonna be here any day, now, I know it. Otherwise, we wouldn't have this stupid evacuation order." A brunette classmate remarked, leaning towards the window a few seats down from where Kaiya sat.

"I don't believe the moon's getting closer. I think the government is just projecting a hologram into the sky to force us to evacuate so they can steal our land." Another student said, out of Kaiya's sight.

"Shut up, Kyle." The brunette scoffed and turned to go back to her seat.

"Did you hear about the evacuation?" A different student said, walking into the classroom with one of her friends.

"Of course I did. You'd have to be living under a rock to not hear about it."

The cacophony of voices grew to a dull roar as more and more students entered the Advanced Biology classroom, all talking at once about the evacuation order.

"Well, my dad thinks that Governor Harvey is a d—"

"This is stupid. I don't want to move out."

"Where are we gonna go?"

"What's going to happen to all of our stuff?"

"Will we ever get to come back?"

"Well, *I* think it's a government setup—"

"Shut *UP, KYLE.*"

RING!

The school bell rang, causing a ripple of jumps throughout the students, their conversations screeching to a halt. Across the room, the classroom door closed shut with a hideous screech of ancient wood on scuffed tile, the doorknob squeaking as it returned to its neutral position.

Framed by the silhouette of the door was Kaiya's Advanced Biology teacher. He was tall and wore a white button-down paired with black slacks. His hair was dark brown with thick grey strands that curled at the ends, just below his brow. Hard lines sculpted his face into a permanent state of aging. His eyes, an emerald green, were shadowed as if a veil had descended over them.

Mr. White, the only Advanced Biology teacher at Atlantic High School, cleared his throat to reign in his class of seniors.

"Good morning, class. Before we start our unit on geology, I want to touch on Governor Harvey's evacuation order, as I'm sure most of you have heard news of." Mr. White said, his baritone voice immediately quieting the low hum of student whispers. He paused and looked around the room, surveying the young adults before him, his eyes seeming to skip over Kaiya.

"Regardless of your political ideologies or skepticism otherwise, Governor Harvey's decision to evacuate coastal Maine is necessary for the survival and safety of the people. I understand the commotion; believe me, I do. Leaving home is no small feat, especially for those who have lived near Niboiwi Bay your entire life." Mr. White paused, reaching up with his right hand to graze a golden pendant that hung around his neck. A flower?

"As I'm sure you are all aware, the cause of this evacuation is not something that is meant to be taken lightly. It is in your best interest to start preparing as soon as possible. The scientific community has declared a state of emergency, with few viable solutions to our… growing problem."

Does he think we've been living under a rock for the past five years?

"Even though this isn't Mrs. Kellem's Astronomy class down the hall, you all must know and see the effects that the moon has on life on Earth. From the tides to animals' mating cycles to weather, they are all heavily influenced by the moon. As you all will remember, a few months ago, scientists deemed the moon's proximity to Earth had affected Earth's gravity to a noticeable degree, such that you all shouldn't be complaining so much about heavy backpacks."

The class laughed, a wave of pitches and voices that

pushed all other thoughts out of Kaiya's head. She shut her eyes tightly, mentally blockading her ears from the stimulus.

This isn't real.

"There are scientists working day and night to adjust the moon's orbital path back to its original course in the sky. For now, however, we have to comply with the Governor's mandate to evacuate by June 29th. Thankfully, this will be after your graduation. Think of it as a senior trip!" Mr. White smiled, but it didn't quite reach his eyes. The tense atmosphere of the classroom seemed to ease at his gesture, the students letting out a collective breath they had been unconsciously holding in.

How can he be joking at a time like this....? Shouldn't Mr. White, of all people, show more concern about the growing tides?

"Now that *that* is out of the way, let's get started on today's lesson." Mr. White turned towards the clouded chalkboard, a permanent shade of grey from years of chalky writing. He reached up with his arm and started writing the title for the day's lesson, *Intro to Geology*.

Rocks aren't alive. This is stupid. Isn't this biology? Living biology??

"To start our lesson today, we are going to be learning about the visual differences between igneous, sedimentary, and metamorphic rocks and how the environment can affect those features." The hollow knocking of chalk against the board set the tempo of the classroom, while the rustling of papers and pencils against the student's desks created an academic melody.

Kaiya leaned down towards her backpack that sat on the floor next to her desk. She started unzipping the largest pocket, pulling at the seams. The fabric was worn, originally a bright cerulean, now a faded blue-gray. The zipper caught for a moment, stubborn against Kaiya's fingers.

Across the room came a knocking at the classroom door.

Probably just a late student.

The zipper was incredibly persistent, locking away Kaiya's notebook from her prying hands. She heard the door open but didn't see who walked in.

"Alrighty, class. I would like you all to give a warm welcome to our new student, Bo, who will be finishing out the year with us." Mr. White said, supposedly gesturing to the new student.

The class responded with a chorus of, "Hi, Bo!" With a few "Welcome, Bo!" peppered in with the greetings. Kaiya mumbled a quick, "Hey, Bo," under her breath as she struggled to open her backpack. She glanced up for a moment and watched a girl wearing a grey sweatshirt sit down towards the back of the class. Her hood was up, so Kaiya couldn't see Bo's face as she sat down.

She seems like she'd be pretty.

When Bo turned to set down her backpack, Kaiya caught a glimpse of her face from across the room. She had dark brown skin with her hair in tight twists that fell just below her chin. Her eyes were almond-shaped and housed golden honey irises, invoking images of tomes of gold-lined books. She looked like the ending song of a coming-of-age film, crescendos of emotion, contentedness.

For just a moment, Bo and Kaiya locked eyes, their hands both fiddling with their respective backpacks. Kaiya tilted her head to the side and smiled, a seemingly automatic response that awoke Kaiya from her despondent thoughts. Something about Bo was familiar, like she had seen her in a dream some time ago.

Bo's eyes widened at the sight of Kaiya, a sign of recognition? But behind Bo's eyes was something less friendly, fearful, a sort of apprehension danced behind her irises. Bo quickly looked away and pulled her hood further in front of her face.

Weird. Maybe she's just shy?

Kaiya shook away the interaction, a dream, a memory? Deja vu? She turned back towards the board where Mr. White was drawing a tri-Venn diagram with the labels igneous, sedimentary, and metamorphic next to each overlapping circle. Surely enough, a lecture on rocks was enough to distract Kaiya from the new student.

"Okay, class. Who can tell me the difference between each kind of rock? Or, more simply, what can physically change the appearance of each type of rock?" Mr. White promptly finished writing and turned on his heel to face his students.

The classroom stayed silent, with some students already asleep with their heads tucked into their arms on the desks.

"Anyone?" Mr. White asked, set the piece of chalk down on a ledge, and then leaned up against his desk.

Still, silence.

"Early morning, huh? Well," Mr. White turned back towards the board again, chalk in hand, and started writing inside the intersection between the three circles.

Is this really necessary? It's not like I need to be able to identify rocks by their looks. Aren't we not supposed to judge a book by its cover? Why are we judging rocks by their surfaces, huh?

She's got a point.

"First off," Mr. White continued, still turned towards the board, "is one of the most obvious natural factors." He turned back towards the class, a last-ditch attempt to acknowledge voluntary student participation.

"Water," Mr. White pointed out the window towards Niboiwi Bay, then turned and wrote 'WATER' in large letters in the center of the Venn diagram. "The universal solvent, as I'm sure you all remember from one of our first units this year." Some students started writing down the notes while others simply watched the biology teacher write across the chalkboard.

Kaiya pulled out a piece of paper from her bag, the zipper finally complying with her fingers' advances to open it. In the middle of the paper, using her finest cursive, she wrote the word 'WATER' in large, curling letters. The tip of her pen moved with a vigor of its own, trailing ink from the end bump of the 'R' into a cresting wave. An ocean coming to life on the page.

"Gravity and pressure also aid in the formation of rocks. The degree of pressure is different for the different categories, but pressure nonetheless directly affects the physical appearance of stones." Underneath 'WATER,' Mr. White wrote 'PRESSURE' and 'GRAVITY.' in the Venn Diagram's center.

"Can anyone guess what the last factor is?" The biology teacher faced the class, scanning the young faces for some sense of understanding.

The room stayed quiet. After a moment, Mr. White slowly swiveled back towards the board and gave a small sigh, almost mistakable for a whisper of wind, which conveyed the shallow disappointment in his voice.

"Heat? Or intense light?" A sweet molasses voice chimed up quietly from the back of the classroom. Mr. White, along with the other seniors in class, spun around to see the brave soul who answered a question on a bleak Monday morning during the peak of senioritis season.

Clearly not used to the attention, Bo slid further into her seat, her grey hoodie covering most of her face.

"Wonderful, Bo! Thank you for answering the final factor in the creation of stone's appearances." Mr. White beamed, clearly ecstatic to hear another person speak during his seven am class of seniors battling an environmental crisis and science finals. He filled up the rest of the Venn Diagram's middle section with the words 'HEAT' and 'LIGHT' in large, blocky letters. With a final scrape of the chalk, Mr. White crossed off the T and returned his attention to the class.

"You're all probably thinking, 'Mr. White, why should I ever need to know what causes rocks to look different?' And to that, I will tell you that the Advanced Biology Exam creators love to throw in a few questions about geology during the final, so you can all thank me later when you get to those questions on the exam and know the answers!" Mr. White grinned, the smile finally seeming to reach his eyes.

No wonder he decided to be a teacher. He clearly loves kids...
RING!

"Ope! Well, that's the bell then. I will see you all bright and early tomorrow, and we will discuss the geological processes of the formation of different types of rocks. Bye, guys! Have a good day!" Mr. White said, a quarter of his students had already packed up and out the door.

Kaiya shoved her paper back into her bag, her pencil already buried underneath her binders and notebooks. When she looked up again, however, the one person she was trying to find had already left.

Humph. I guess I'll just have to try and find Bo again tomorrow. I feel like I should talk to her.

One more scan around the room confirmed Kaiya's notion that Bo had already left the classroom. Without another thought, Kaiya picked up her backpack and slung it over her shoulder. She walked up the aisle between the desks and briskly pushed her way through the door into the crowded hallway, avoiding all eye contact as she moved.

From his solitary chair behind his desk, Mr. White's gaze followed Kaiya as she left his classroom, a soft film of tears sheathing his turquoise eyes.

VI.

The fading rays of sunset streamed in through the Greenhouse panes, casting a sleepy glow onto the overgrown garden. Vines caressed the wooden posts that supported the glass ceiling; spiderwebs of cracks pierced the areas under the most pressure. Nothing too dangerous, though, don't worry. Hanging out under an unstable glass ceiling was the least of Kaiya's worries.

When Kaiya was younger, Mrs. Abbott would use the Greenhouse as an outdoor studio. She would crack open the windows and splash paint over the inside rims of the glass. These painted frames had long since peeled away, the previous real estate taken over by moss and creeping vines. Once upon a time, Kaiya was the sole subject of Mrs. Abbott's photography.

Not so much anymore.

Since then, the far corner of the greenhouse had been cleared of vines and broken glass. Bright tapestries of mandalas, red, orange, and yellow, hung from the horizontal wooden beams of the ceiling. A few homemade suncatchers of ruptured glass and old jewelry hung from nails, casting colored light from their broken edges. A purple circular floor pillow separated Kaiya from the cold stone tile. Papers and notebooks were strewn about the pillow, some spilling over onto the stone floor, an organized chaos of academia.

Kaiya's primary focus of the night was her biology test, which was the following Monday. Normally, Kaiya would spend her Friday evenings after school at the beach, searching. If anything, walking along the shore barefoot seemed to steep away her anxieties through her soles, the Earth tucking away Kaiya's worries into her molten core.

Mr. White had sailed through the geology unit at light speed, using only five class periods to explain the complexities of rock formation, the Earth's layers, and the rock cycle.

Yes. The rock cycle is a real thing. Who knew?

Since Mr. White had moved so fast, Kaiya was struggling to remember all of the material. It didn't help that her concussion all those years ago had royally damaged her ability to recall information. So, instead of visiting the Niboiwi shore, Kaiya was holed up in her corner of the Greenhouse, studying.

Dusk had started to fall, swallowing up the rainbows cast from the suncatchers and enveloping Kaiya's world in darker tones. Past the sharp edges of the greenhouse beams, somewhere out of sight, was Niboiwi Bay and that Atlantic Ocean, lapping against the shore. Somewhere, hidden between the barks of the trees or the crevices of the stones, was a clue. A hint of someone long gone but not left behind.

Overhead was the moon, her large surface taking up about a third of the sky. The moonlight was just bright enough to show the contrast between Kaiya's black-penned handwriting and the stark whiteness of the lined paper. The gradual descent of night had led Kaiya's eyes to adjust to the dim lighting, even if she was squinting a little. She was so focused on her notes, the tip of her pencil's eraser in her mouth, to notice the quiet shuffling of footsteps against the greenhouse's stone floor.

"You'll need glasses at this rate." Mrs. Abbott said, only slightly annoyed, thankfully. Kaiya's study session ended with a jolt.

"I just need a few more minutes to review stones' physical attributes, then I'll come back inside. I'm sorry I haven't walked Blaine yet today." Kaiya blurted in response, already preparing herself for her mother's daily berating.

"Well, I'm glad to see that you at least are *aware* that you have responsibilities in this house." Mrs. Abbott remarked, which was code for *Do what I ask now before I have to bring your Father into it.* She looked up and down Kaiya's study space, her lip curling into a shape of disgust. Mrs. Abbott fiddled with her fingers, absentmindedly picking at her nails until her hands eventually laid to rest on the sides of her neon paint-splattered overalls. It looked like one of those neon *OPEN* signs had combusted all over Mrs. Abbott's clothes. The childish look of her apparel almost seemed to deepen the lines of age across her face and hands.

Kaiya remained quiet, knowing all too well that

a response would have only encouraged her mother to embark on a long, guilt-tripping tangent. She started slowly packing up her notes, organizing them in a neat pile to be tucked away into her backpack. Anything to extend her time spent in the greenhouse under the light of the moon.

"Oh, come on, Kaiya. Hurry up. You still have to walk Blaine, and I brought some boxes up to your room from the basement. If you don't look through them now, I will have them taken to the dump. You need to start thinking about what you want to take and what you want to leave behind." Mrs. Abbott clapped, urging Kaiya to hurry, before she turned on her heel and walked out the door, pausing every few feet to stand in awe-struck disgust at the unkempt vegetation.

Kaiya watched her mother walk out, knowing that she wouldn't turn around to look back at her daughter. She sighed and finished pulling together the rest of her school supplies. No more streaks of sunlight were left in the sky, so Kaiya navigated the stone floor of the greenhouse by moonlight. She could have walked out with her eyes closed, but one too many haphazardly trips on vines had deterred Kaiya from doing so.

On her right, a blacktop driveway snaked back into the forest. A navy sedan sat parked outside the embellished garage doors. A singular lamppost shone artificial sunlight over the entrance to the Abbott's Home.

Kaiya's house was nestled between the forest, the sea, and the sky. The front door faced east; its windows would capture the morning light of the sun over the distant horizon of the Atlantic Ocean. Though the land was old, the house itself was built in a more modern sense. Tall, white pillars, simple, wound up towards the high apex of the roof. The angled ledges of the house showed prestige and dominance over the organic scenery surrounding it.

After strolling through the crunchy, dry grass, Kaiya used her foot to kick open the clasp to the fancy front door handle. The clean, pearly white door had permanent scuff marks right below the brass knob. Of the exterior of the house, the marks were the only perceivable abnormalities on its surface. She could've used her hands like a normal person, but the small action annoyed Mrs. Abbott, so Kaiya never stopped the habit.

The foyer of the Abbott House was simple yet abstract. Cream walls set the background for golden-framed art; bright strokes of neons and silhouettes of long-lost figures adorned the walls. Above, a delicate chandelier of thousands of crystals refracted light from an even higher skylight that pierced the angled roof.

Kaiya kicked off her shoes, not particularly caring where they landed. She shut the door with her hip and yelled down the hall.

"Blaine? C'mere, girl!" Kaiya knelt and patted her knees, calling out to her dog.

The distant sound of scratching paws against hardwood grew louder as Blaine bolted around the corner. Her feet slipped out beneath her, and she slammed into the foyer wall, quickly recovering back onto her paws to resume the pursuit. By the time Blaine reached Kaiya's arms, she was just a flurry of white-haired Samoyed.

"Hey, girl! How's my little baby doing?" Kaiya cooed at her fluffy puppy.

Yes. Kaiya knows that Blaine is about four years

past "baby" age. Does she care?

Of course not.

Blaine pounced on Kaiya, knocking her backward with fifty pounds of force. She licked Kaiya's face until it glistened with slobber, an affectionate yet sometimes overbearing gesture. The seventeen-year-old giggled as she wrapped her arms around Blaine's torso. A puff of white fur sank slowly towards the ground.

"Aww, is my baby shedding?" Kaiya cocked her head to the side as Blaine mirrored her. The Samoyed's tail wagged back and forth, her ears perked up, looking satisfied with herself.

"It's only May! Let's go comb you out—"

Down the bend of the hallway, Mr. Abbott cleared his voice.

Oh no.

Mr. Abbott appeared in the frame of the foyer. To see him without a suit jacket on was a rarity. His hands rested in his black slack's pockets, surely in fists. Mr. Abbott is clean-shaven and framed with closely trimmed ebony hair. The only organic thing about him was his freckles. His face barely showed his age since wrinkles did not adorn the corners of his eyes. A smile from Kaiya's father was a rather jubilant occasion, indeed.

"You're late for dinner, and you still haven't started on your chores. Go sit down." Mr. Abbott said, looking towards the skylight. He didn't have a look of concern, care, or worry; he just simply looked up, not meeting his daughter's eyes.

"I'm sorry. It won't happen again." Kaiya rose from the ground as Blaine trotted into the kitchen, passing Mr.

Abbott on her way. Though she tried to catch his eye, Mr. Abbott stayed gazing out the window, a pale light slowly illuminating his skin.

Kaiya shuffled through the foyer, past her father, into the kitchen. Though she didn't look back herself, she knew exactly what the subject of her father's gaze was.

The moon.

Who wouldn't be looking at the moon?

Many a sleepover with Opal was spent gazing into the night sky. Though the pair would typically focus more on constellations, constantly quizzing each other on their names and origins, the two always made sure to pay their respects to the moon. They admired her heavenly glow that, when full, could turn even the darkest of nights into day. Even now, years after Opal's disappearance, Kaiya would search the stars for some sort of sign that her best friend was still out there.

"Sit down, Kaiya. Your food is getting cold." Mrs. Abbott's voice jostled Kaiya from her memory.

"Sorry, Mom," Kaiya said, shuffling towards the long rectangular dinner table. One end of the table had two plates set upon light blue placemats. The largest plate sat at the head of the table, but no one sat behind it. Mr. Abbott, it seemed, was still gazing through the foyer's skylight.

The second plate sat to the right of the head of the table. Mrs. Abbott, a frail woman with even daintier features, sat behind the secondary plate. The portion of food on her plate mimicked her stature, tiny portions that simply could not fill the mighty plate they sat on. Mrs. Abbott's hair was the darkest of the family, possibly aided by the Niboiwin ancestry she so dearly held on to. Around her neck lay a moonstone wrapped in elaborate copper wire; its opalesque surface would shine the occasional rainbow across Mrs. Abbott's dark pantsuits she would wear at her art exhibitions. Supposedly, it was a gift passed down from her Great-Great-Great-Grandmother, the head Chieftess of the Niboiwin Tribe, for which the bay is also named. Her skin, however, did not inherit the native glow that Niboiwins were so known for. It stretched across her high cheekbones like a trampoline pulled too tight for its frame.

The third plate, however, sat the furthest distance away from the head of the table. A small plate, a piece chipped off from some sort of accident or another, lay empty. No placemat protected the plate from the mahogany dinner table.

Kaiya grabbed her plate and turned away from the table as her father entered the kitchen with resounding *thuds* of his business shoes. With swift movements, Kaiya forked a portion of grilled salmon onto her plate, next scooping up mashed potatoes to accompany the fish. When Kaiya looked up again, the glowing television in the living room caught her eye.

Some newscaster, an older man, was on the screen showing pictures of seaside towns that were beginning to sink under the waves of the ocean, the moon looming large in the distance of the camera shot.

"The city of Acadia is experiencing rising sea levels and is being urged to evacuate earlier than the Governor's June twenty-ninth deadline. Docks are beginning to fall beneath the salty seawater while high tide creeps higher and higher up the shores of the small town. Experts say—"

Kaiya heard snippets of what the newscaster said as she slunk behind her father's chair.

Experts this, experts that. If there are so many experts, why isn't there a solution yet?

"Just the same news that's always on. Hon," Mrs. Abbott said to her husband, who was busy filling his own plate. "Did you see that we should be watching out for more... dead animals? Something about how there's more light at night from the moon, so little mice and things can't hide as well. I would hate for you to come into contact with any of those vermin. God forbid you or Blaine get rabies."

"I hadn't heard about that, dear." Mr. Abbott replied curtly, rounding the corner of the island to take his seat at the head of the table.

Kaiya had turned to face her mother, showing that she was listening, but she had not taken a step to sit down. Steam swirled up from her plate of food.

"Kaiya, sit down. What are you standing around for?" Mr. Abbott remarked irritably.

"I, uhm," Kaiya paused, wanting anything but to sit down at a family dinner.

"'Uhm,' what? Words, please." Mr. Abbott replied, lightly tapping the tip of his knife on the mahogany table.

"I... I was just wondering if I could eat upstairs tonight," Kaiya stumbled out, almost too fast to be comprehensible. "Mother asked me to look through some boxes she found."

Mr. Abbott only stared, one eyebrow raised. His gaze turned towards his wife, who seemed to recede back into her chair.

"Well, I did say that, hon. I don't want any more

junk laying around, especially before we move." Mrs. Abbott mumbled, looking down into her salmon.

There was a slight pause, Kaiya looking at her father, him looking at his wife, who only stared into her food. The air turned stale and dry, like day-old bread set out in the sun.

"I don't care. Just make sure to clean up," Mr. Abbott answered, his attention already turned back towards his food.

Kaiya could barely mumble out a "thank you" before she sped out of the kitchen towards the staircase that led to the second floor. She balanced her plate of food

When Kaiya finally pushed open her bedroom door, she let out a breath she didn't realize she was holding in. She turned on her heel and started closing the door, a little white snout peeking through the crack in the doorway before she could close it all the way.

"Cmere, baby. I didn't mean to close the door on you." Kaiya opened the door and whispered. Blaine trotted into the bedroom, her tongue hanging out of her huge smile, clearly happy to see her person.

"Hi, sweetheart. Cmere." Kaiya repeated, holding her arms out as she sat down on the shag carpet floor. Blaine pounced into her arms, enveloping Kaiya in slobbery kisses. Kaiya giggled, a youthful laugh that she hardly made anymore.

"Alrighty, Blaine. Let's see what Mother wants us to look through." Kaiya laughed, gently pushing Blaine off of her chest, and waved over to her bed. Despite Blaine's four years of age, she bounded up onto the pink covers of Kaiya's bed with puppy-like vigor.

Piled haphazardly on Kaiya's twin-sized bed were three large boxes, each labeled with scrawling thick markers that read *KAIYA'S KEEPSAKES* in large letters. Long forgotten mementos from a bygone era, one filled to the brim with love and care.

Oh boy. This should be fun.

Kaiya sighed, and Blaine tilted her head at Kaiya, her ears pricking up at the sound of dismay. The black-haired girl leaned down and scratched Blaine's ears. A sort of preparation for the emotional toil that was sure to spill out of the boxes as soon as she unfolded the cardboard flaps.

Her fingers hesitated on the rough edge of the cardboard box, contemplating whether or not to open it tonight.

Mother will throw it all out otherwise...
I have to do this. Now.

Kaiya let out a low breath. She picked at the edge of the folded lid, slowly creasing the cardboard to pull apart the flaps. A cloud of dust poofed up from the box as Kaiya smoothed the flaps flush to its sides. On the very top of the box was a blush pink baby blanket embroidered with colorful butterflies, ladybugs, and flowers. In the center of the blanket was Kaiya's name in sprawling cursive blue lettering. The edges of the soft blanket were lined with silk, a few holes peppering the stitching from years of use.

She reached out towards the blanket, her fingers curling around the silk edges. Kaiya lifted the blanket up to her cheek, turning her nose into the fabric and closing her eyes. The soft divots of the embroidery added just enough stimulation to remind Kaiya of her mother's hands, small and slightly calloused. The blanket smelled like rosehip oil, the same scent as Mrs. Abbott's arthritis hand cream.

When Kaiya opened her eyes again, the comfort melted away, sliding back down to cover her memories in a rosy glow. The time had long since passed for Kaiya to sleep with her baby blanket. That time in her life was tucked away into cardboard boxes and scrapbooks.

Kaiya gently folded the baby blanket and set it on the edge of her bed. Blaine leaned over and rested her head on the blankets, her white fur already starting to cover the pink silk.

"You ready for the next layer, Blaine?" Kaiya cooed, kneeling down to be eye level with her Samoyed. Blaine started wagging her tail back and forth, brushing the wall behind her as she wagged, her head tilted to the side with curiosity.

"Alrighty, then." Kaiya patted her legs and stood back up. She turned back towards the first open box and peered inside. There was a purple photo album, a pair of small ballet shoes, some baby clothes, and a porcelain doll. Kaiya leaned over and gingerly picked up the doll from her box home. The doll looked almost identical to Kaiya when she was younger: tan skin with long dark hair, freckles, and her slanted Niboiwi nose that she got from her mother, dressed in a pale lilac dress. Yet, the doll's eyes were bright blue with a golden ring around the irises. A family heirloom passed down from her mother's side, almost identical to Kaiya, except for the eyes.

Kaiya gazed into the doll's eyes for a moment, the memories of playing with her flooding back. Opal had a wonderful dollhouse in her basement that Kaiya would bring her doll to play with. Once, those shining blue and gold eyes had seen two best friends playing house together. Now, the only thing those eyes had seen in the past couple of years was the inside of a box.

She turned and set the doll softly onto her pillow, out of harm's way. Kaiya looked back into the box and pulled out the purple photo album. It fit snugly into her palm; the cover was smooth plastic which contrasted the blunt edges of the photo sheets. Kaiya's fingers ran over the spine of the photobook, finally hooking her finger inside the cover to flip open the album.

The photos were, at best, about four inches wide and six inches tall. The album housed about one hundred photo sheets, pictures displayed in the front and back cellophane sleeves. Kaiya flipped through the pictures, watching herself grow through the pages. Newborn into a toddler, her first steps immortalized in a flash. There was a photo of Kaiya's first day of kindergarten. The straps of her Hello Kitty backpack looked comically large on her small shoulders.

Mother had picked that backpack out for me...

Kindergarten transformed into grade school as Kaiya flipped through the photo sheets. Family reunions and birthday parties dotted the timeline as Kaiya grew. The photo album grew blurry. Not from the camera's quality, no. Tears started to cloud Kaiya's eyes, the nostalgia of what once was setting off the waterworks.

Kaiya's fingers paused on one of the photos towards the back half of the album. It was a bright photo of the beach, the sun slightly overexposing the white summer sand. Mr. Abbott was knee-deep in the water and *smiling*.

His arms were outstretched, with little Kaiya hanging onto his hands. The edges of the father-daughter duo blurred due to their spinning movement. Kaiya, who must've been about twelve at the time, was laughing, her mouth wide open in a toothy grin. Her eyes were squinted shut to shield them from the salty sea spray.

Can I get this version of him back?

She hesitated to turn the page, fearing that Mr. Abbott's smile would never return if she covered the photo.

Why did he have to turn so bitter?

Kaiya finally turned the page, her father's smiling face turning away with it. The next page was another picture from that same summer. Three figures huddled together in front of the rocky coastline, a cliff looming high in the background. Their arms were wrapped tightly around each other, their cheeks touching together. Three faces of glittering smiles, their teeth only slightly crooked and adorned with braces.

In the center of the trio was Opal, her blonde hair streaked with pink and glitter.

She dyed streaks of her hair pink for her twelfth birthday. I know, since I bought her the hair dye.

Kaiya stood to the right of Opal. Her skin was much darker than it is now, considering she spent almost every day outside exploring with her best friend. Kaiya was a whole head taller than Opal, but she had bent down so that their cheeks touched.

However, Kaiya didn't recognize the person on Opal's left.

At least, not at first.

The girl on Opal's left had dark skin and these large,

beautiful honey golden eyes. Her hair was tied back into box braids with rainbow beads adorning the ends. Her arm was wrapped around Opal, but it didn't quite reach Kaiya.

There's only one other person in Acadia that has eyes like that.

Bo…? That can't be right.

Kaiya closed her eyes, mentally taking herself back to the first day that Bo had shown up to class. She analyzed the curve of her cheekbones, the swoop of her nose, the edges of her lips. When Kaiya opened her eyes again, it was clear as day. Sure, her features were more mature and refined now, but the girl in the photo *had* to be Bo.

We've met before?
And… Bo knew Opal too?

Kaiya dropped the photo album onto her bedroom floor, startling Blaine in the process. The floor started to spin beneath her feet as the moonlight shone through her windows in broken fragments. Blaine scampered towards the head of the bed before Kaiya sat down where Blaine was moments before. Kaiya grabbed her bedframe in an attempt to hold herself upright and still. The back of her head throbbed in the same place that had caused her concussion that dreadful June night.

There was a third? Another girl?
And now she's back?

Jealousy coursed through her veins. Kaiya hadn't felt an emotion this strong since… well. Opal disappeared. But there it was, the green ooze of envy slithering and pumping under her skin, burning hatred behind her eyes, flickering fire at her fingertips. Questions shot through

Kaiya's brain like poisonous darts, their green tails streaking her thoughts with doubt. Is this the only picture of the three girls together? Why wasn't Bo with Kaiya and Opal that night?

And why was she so scared to talk to me in class...
I have to find her.
Now.
Opal's life depends on it.

VII.

Water lapped quietly against the fine sand of Niboiwi beach, the jangle of Blaine's dog tags chiming as she trotted through the damp beach. Hanging just above the tall Ash trees was the slowly setting sun. Within the hour, sharp shadows from the forest would pierce the beach like gnarled teeth, hungry for the depth of the bay.

Although May had been long underway, the weather still seemed to be stuck in a cold spring. A cool wind blew off the waves of the bay, causing Kaiya to zip up her grey windbreaker. One of her hands held a pink metal water bottle, adorned in stickers that had begun to peel at the edges, her other hand stuffed into her pocket. Blaine didn't seem to mind the cold, even if she did look like a poofy cotton ball in the wind.

For once, I wish the weekend would go by faster.
I need to talk to Bo.

Kaiya shivered, but not from the breeze.

Even though the sun still shone over the coast, the moon was already a massive sight on the Eastern horizon. Her circular edges divided the sky into the present and the past, a moving memorial of time as it stood, frozen, and of the memories that were etched into her surface.

It seemed as if Kaiya floated down the coastline, her autopilot kicked in, and she took a back seat to her own body. She had trained her puppy to walk without a leash on, so Kaiya could fall back into her thoughts as they strolled. Blaine was a spry young dog and intelligent too. She knew to stay near Kaiya and could tell when they were on their way back home. Now, however, Blaine turned away from the bay and trotted over to the cliffside, following a new path.

Or at least, new to Blaine.

"Blaine! Where're ya going, sweetheart? We're supposed to be heading back to the house!" Kaiya cupped her hands and yelled. Blaine turned back towards her owner, wagged her tail, and bounded into a sea cave.

Yes. *That* sea cave.

Kaiya sighed, slowly turning on her heel towards the rocky entrance that eventually led to the Atrium. She hadn't slept all that great last night, her slumber plagued with nightmares of cold, rushing water and darkness. The sun would set soon, and Kaiya wasn't looking for another argument with her parents. Despite her exhaustion, she started to jog towards the entrance to the sea cave, her water bottle swinging at her side.

"Blaine? Blaine? Where are you, sweetheart?" Kaiya called down the slate hallway, the channel growing darker with every step. The hushed jingle of Blaine's collar bounced off the slick walls like whispers of encouragement to delve deeper into the cliffside.

This is the last place I want to be in right now.
Who knows what Bo did in here…
To Opal.

Kaiya continued down the hallway, the soft light of dusk emitting from the end to guide her steps. As she approached the entrance to the Atrium, she could hear the quiet scratches of Blaine's paws against the limestone floor.

"Blaine? C'mon, baby, we gotta get back before dark." Kaiya called out as she passed the threshold of the Atrium. It was largely the same as she had left it. Before the evacuation mandate, before Bo showed up. The cave was constant, unchanging, even though Kaiya wished something would change within its walls. A clue, a sign.

Kaiya glanced around the Atrium. A few straggling rays of orange and red filtered down through the skylight, a gentle reminder that night was on its way. Above the shallow pool was a wall covered by white flowers in full bloom. The sedimentary rings along the walls hadn't smudged, and the floors remained a dreadfully dull gray. Large rocks still sat in their heavy seats, unmoving. The scratching sound of Blaine's paws went silent, only to be replaced by the trickling sound of the small flowing stream.

"Blaine…?" Kaiya said, no longer yelling for her puppy but calling out in a harsh whisper, quiet enough that only Blaine would hear. The hair on Kaiya's arms stood on end, her heartbeat drowning out the sound of flowing water.

Kaiya stepped forward out of the safety of the doorway. Out in the open.

"Baby?" Kaiya whispered, her eyes darting around each rock, searching each crevice for her puppy.

From Kaiya's left came a flash of white. Sound rushed back as Kaiya breathed a sigh of relief, time now unfrozen. Blaine bounded over to her owner, her legs poised in a launch position. Before Kaiya could even catch the breath she didn't know she was holding in, Blaine had pounced onto Kaiya's chest, knocking her off her feet. She fell, not as gracefully as she might've wished. Kaiya's sore tailbone was the last thing on her mind, elation spreading like a warm cup of cocoa through her chest. Blaine's paws kept Kaiya pinned to the dusty slate floor as Blaine covered her owner in slobbery kisses.

"You really scared me, Blaine! Don't go running off like that, okay?" Kaiya pleaded, ruffling her fingertips through Blaine's coat. A puff of white fur floated off of her, a messy sign of the warm weather to come. The Samoyed simply cocked her head to the side and wagged her tail, clearly happy with her little excursion.

"Alright, alright, c'mon, baby. Let's get back to the house. It'll be dark by the time we leave." Kaiya said as she gently pushed Blaine off of her. Kaiya moved to lean back against her hands in an effort to sit upright when she felt a cold wetness on her palms. She immediately jerked her hand back from the unknown liquid and whipped around to find the culprit.

Ah, crap.

Kaiya must've dropped her pink water bottle as she was tackled by Blaine. The pink metal exterior lay dented on its side a few feet away, icy water streaming out of the unscrewed cap. Icy water that was starting to soak her pants.

"Crap!" Kaiya scrambled back onto her feet, brushing away the water on her hands onto the sides of her jeans.

Slightly annoyed, Kaiya walked over to her water bottle, now empty, and picked it up, ignoring the water that had spilled onto the floor. She twisted it around in her hands, inspecting the damage. There was a large dent on the top corner, but otherwise, it seemed fine.

"Guess I'll need to invest in a new bottle, huh, Blaine?" Kaiya said as she picked at the flaking pink paint, "Let's get going."

While still examining her water bottle, Kaiya trudged towards the doorway that led back out to the beach. When Kaiya didn't hear Blaine's pitter-patter behind her, she turned around.

"Blaine? You coming?" She said, turning around to see what had caught the puppy's attention. Blaine remained in the center of the Atrium, just under the light of the moon through the skylight. The soft white moon rays illuminated a circle on the ground, right where Kaiya's water had spilled. No longer gray and dusty, the ground where the water was had turned a lighter grey with streaks of sky blue scorches amidst the cloudy surface.

Blaine just stared back at Kaiya, wagging her tail back and forth. She was smiling as if to say, "Look what I found!"

Kaiya inched towards the circle, every muscle in her body tense. Cortisol rushed through her bloodstream, pumping, pumping, pumping. She held her breath as she crept back into the Atrium.

Is this the clue I've been looking for...?

Balancing on her tiptoes, Kaiya edged her way around the circumference of the circular water mark. Blaine followed tight on Kaiya's heels, obviously not understanding the gravity of what she had just found.

Up close, more details of the rock came to light. The light blue streaks were not random, nor could they have been a natural part of the rock. It seemed like the streaks, all going in the same direction, had been blocked out by a figure.

A human-shaped figure.

Oh... my god.

Kaiya knelt down and reached out towards the floor, her hand shaking as she made contact with the ground. It was damp and grainy, the dust that had formerly coated the floor now a chalky paste that ran down towards the shallow pool. Though unassuming to the naked eye, there were many divets and grooves in the rock, almost as if the rock had been melted away. Aside from the blue scorch marks, the area within view of the skylight was much lighter than the surrounding stone, as if it had been bleached by some sort of light.

What happened here...?

Kaiya closed her eyes and shook her head, a vain attempt to shut out the worst-case scenarios. How else do you explain a human-shaped silhouette of scorch marks?

When she opened her eyes again, she felt that Blaine wasn't beside her anymore.

Kaiya jumped to her feet and whipped around. Her eyesight was blurry, tears clouding up her vision. She rubbed her eyes and turned, seeing a flash of white running towards the entrance.

Running away from her, leaving something behind.

Blaine's collar lay at Kaiya's feet.

"Wait! Wait, baby, come back!" Kaiya immediately broke out into a sprint, scooping up Blaine's collar as she dashed towards the doorway.

Kaiya bulldozed her way through the pitch-black halls, her feet unsure of where to step to push her forward, stumbling in the dark. Her blood flushed fast, her heart beating through her ears. The walls were slick with moisture as Kaiya's skin grew slick with sweat.

"Stop! Please!" Kaiya screamed, plunging through the dark. She started to lose feeling in her fingers, her iron grip on Blaine's collar unrelenting.

I can't lose you, too.

Kaiya strained her ears, trying to pick up the smallest sound to indicate that Blaine wasn't too far ahead of her. The soft scratching of Blaine's paws receded as she gained distance on Kaiya.

Light.

White moonlight shone through the end of the tunnel, illuminating the rocks and the sea beyond. Kaiya kept racing even though every muscle in her body begged her to stop. Her limbs felt thick and heavy, like weights that her soul dragged behind her.

The light was blinding as Kaiya burst into the night air. She stopped and whipped around until she spotted Blaine dashing down the beach, about a hundred feet away.

Lactic acid saturated her body, her lungs screaming for more oxygen.

I can't catch up.

Kaiya collapsed in the sand, her legs refusing to hold her body. Without a thought, Kaiya screeched at the top of her lungs.

"BLAIR!" Kaiya drawled out until she didn't have any breath left to scream.

Blair...?

Kaiya's vision went dark, memories starting to flash by her eyelids like a movie screen. The third girl from the photo was there, yelling, crying, storming away. Bo had ran away on this very beach.

Bo's real name... is Blair?

Blaine turned around at the name just as she reached the dark tree line.

Why would she change her name? Why was she running away? Where did Blair go, and why couldn't I remember her? Why, why, why, why, WHY?

Kaiya threw her head into her hands, trying to drown out the questions in her head. Her breathing grew heavy, the sand swirling around Kaiya's knees as she hyperventilated.

She stayed like that, rocking herself in the sand for what felt like ages. Panic tends to twist time like that. Eventually, however, Blaine poked her nose in between Kaiya's tightly crossed arms.

Kaiya didn't say another word. As soon as she felt Blaine was near, Kaiya's arms wrapped around her puppy like a spring trap. She deftly clipped Blaine's collar back around her furry neck and twisted it around, so the tags lay across her chest. After a moment of furry embrace, Kaiya was able to breathe again.

"C'mon, baby. It's late," Kaiya cupped the sides of

Blaine's face to look her in her bright blue eyes. "Let's get you home."

Kaiya slowly rose to her feet and brushed the sand off of her clothes. With Blaine trotting next to her, the two made their way down the beach, back towards Abbott Hill.

Meanwhile, Mrs. Abbott watched her daughter from the safety of the greenhouse, her brows furrowed in recognition of a name long since forgotten.

VIII.

Friday, May twenty-ninth, 2020. Exactly one month left before the Governor's evacuation mandate became permanent.

Bo hasn't been in class at all this week.
There's no way that she knows that I know her secret.
Right…?

Kaiya shuffled into her first period. Mr. White was sitting at his desk, clicking away at his computer. The heavy round clock on the wall tick, tick, ticked, slowly running out of sand.

The bell rang as Kaiya took her seat. A flood of other seniors rushed to their desks, knowing all too well that Mr. White would mark them tardy if they weren't sitting by the end of the morning announcements. Kaiya's eyes surveyed the room, only one face on her mind.

Where are you…?

Bo's desk in the back corner of the classroom sat

empty.

Go figure.

The first time in five years I actually have a lead, and she doesn't show up?

Kaiya played with her hair, twisting it between her fingers. Her leg bounced on the tip of her toes. Outside the window, rain poured down from dark, overbearing rainclouds. The sidewalk outside steamed as the droplets pelted the hot pavement. Beyond the pavement, along the treeline, was a group of red-shouldered hawks converged on a mischief of dead mice, feeding. They just couldn't adapt fast enough to the newfound light of the moon.

I guess I won't have to worry about mice in the hallways now, huh?

The announcements rambled on, the principal reciting dates of exams and warning students about consistent absences. Kaiya's eyes remained on the hawks, their feathers soaking with rain. A pink stream of diluted blood ran down the length of the pavement, eventually filtering out into the grass.

"Alrighty, class. Let's get started on our review for our geology unit next class." Mr. White said, breaking the silence after the announcements had finished. He walked down each row of students, handing out review packets as he went.

Knock, knock.

Mr. White stopped handing out packets and turned on his heel towards the door.

Bo?

Kaiya leaned forward in her chair, the sharp edge of the desk poking into her ribs. Her eyes were trained on

80

the door like a sniper through a scope, not even blinking. Mr. White approached the doorway and reached out with his free hand to open the door.

A brunette senior who only ever spoke to leave the class walked through the open entryway, mumbling a sarcastic apology for her tardiness.

Thunk.

The solid wooden desk reverberated with the force of Kaiya's forehead.

Goddamnit.
She's not here.
Again.

Kaiya's head remained face-down on her desk, the darkness of her eyelids trying to coo her back to sleep. She wrapped her arms around her head in an effort to shield her disappointment.

Sleep would be so much better than being here.

"Could you hand this to… her." A voice, most likely Mr. White's, whispered to a student a few feet away from Kaiya. Light breached her cave of solitude as someone slid a thick paper packet in between her arm and the desk.

"Thanks," Kaiya mumbled, head still in her arms, not even bothering to look at the student next to her who had given her the review.

He couldn't even bring himself to hand me a review sheet. Lovely.

At the front of the classroom, Mr. White began flipping through the review packet, talking over the key points as he went. Sometimes, a few students would ask questions. Not many, though. It was probable that Kaiya wasn't the only student with her head down. Mr. White had just grown to ignore the students who didn't pay attention in his class. The world was ending, so… what was the point?

Kaiya's head remained sandwiched between her arms and the desk. Questions raced through her mind, some coherent, others not, but questions nonetheless.

What happened to the floor in the Atrium? The scorches?
Why did I call Blaine 'Blair?'
What did Bo do to Opal?

Mr. White lectured on, his voice muffled through the fibers of Kaiya's black sweatshirt. Time inched on, her mind a messy collage of red string connections, overlapped by a geology lecture.

RING!

"Alrighty, guys. Remember, we test next class! Make sure to study those stones! And remember, no matter the score, you guys rock!" Mr. White said, the class groaning at his rock pun.

Kaiya finally raised her head from between her arms. Pins and needles wracked up her hands and forearms, her skin feeling like static on a television. When Kaiya opened her eyes again, the fluorescent light of the classroom shot off of the lightbulbs in blurry streaks. She rubbed her eyes until her vision returned to the crystal clear classroom in front of her. As she turned to grab her backpack, a figure in grey sweats and twist-outs flashed by the Biology classroom door.

Bo!

Kaiya quickly zipped up her backpack and raced out of the classroom, almost tripping as black spots dotted her vision.

Goddamn iron deficiency.

Her head whipped around the hallway, students blocking the way like a clogged artery. Two doors denoted the end of the hall, and a bright red fluorescent EXIT sign hung above the doors. Just beneath the exit sign was Bo.

Found you.

Kaiya pushed through the horde of students, the kids eventually stepping aside for her steamrolling endeavor. Her grey backpack thwacked against students as she sped towards the EXIT sign, her eyes never leaving Bo's figure. Bo was nonchalantly leaned up against the brick wall, phone in hand; she even seemed to be smiling. Completely oblivious to the rain of terror that plowed towards her.

"*Bo!*" Kaiya demanded, a little louder than she had anticipated. Some students turned at the loud voice, but most of them trucked on, their earbuds blocking out all other sounds.

Bo looked up from her phone and met Kaiya's eyes, only an arms-length apart. Fire burned behind Kaiya's eyes, yet Bo remained still, calm. She looked like the Mona Lisa, her skin much darker but had that same small, mysterious smile etched into their faces.

The two stared at each other. A bead of sweat ran down Kaiya's forehead, steam practically rolling off of her body. Bo stood grounded, unmoving and stoic in the face of a tsunami of rage.

Kaiya opened her mouth to speak, breathing in harshly. Before she could force a word out, Bo grabbed the hood of Kaiya's sweatshirt and yanked her into the nook of the doorway, under the light of the EXIT sign.

"Meet me after school by the edge of the tree line

behind the baseball field. We can talk then." Bo whispered harshly into Kaiya's ear, her face bathed in a red glow, not wasting a moment before dashing away like a dust storm. Here one minute, and gone the next.

. ☽ § ☾ .

The rain had lightened up since Kaiya had first arrived at school, but the remnants of the storm were evident in the saturated ground. Unfortunately, soggy dirt behind the baseball field was the trade-off for privacy with Bo. Kaiya hesitated before stepping off of the concrete into the squishy river of mud beside the sidewalk.

Ugh. I need answers, or I would just go home.

Kaiya tightened the straps on her backpack and put her weight back on her haunches. After mentally preparing herself for the splash of mud and whatever information lay on the other side, Kaiya pushed off of the concrete into the grass just before the treeline. She landed with only a minimal amount of mud on her black canvas shoes.

I should've joined track.

Not only could I do the long jump, but I'm also fantastic at running away from my emotions.

Ha. Good one, brain.

Suddenly, a hand grabbed the handle of Kaiya's backpack, yanking her behind a thick Ash tree. She squealed, which would have been an abrupt interruption of her sarcastic inner conversation if it weren't for the hand that was smacked over her mouth.

"Be quiet. The hawks might hear you," Bo whispered into Kaiya's ear, her head resting on Kaiya's shoulder. The hot air of Bo's breath against Kaiya's skin gave her goosebumps, but not in a frightening way. More similar to the ocean hesitating before crashing upon the shore, water either whisking the sand away or being swallowed by the grains.

Kaiya nodded, Bo's hand still pressed against her lips. Seeing this as an adequate sign of agreement, Bo's hand snaked back to her side.

After slowly turning around, Kaiya eyed Bo up and down, an evaluation of sorts. The girl in front of her was most certainly the same girl in the photo of the trio. She had the same large, honey golden eyes and plump lips, though her jawline was sharper now, more defined.

"So. Are you going to tell me what you did to Opal?" Kaiya managed, her stomach a hurricane of doubt and fear of what would come next.

"First off, just call me Blair. That is my real name, after all. Blair Otieno, hence the nickname, *Bo*," Blair said, crossing her arms over her chest. "I knew that you got a concussion after Opal disappeared, but I didn't think it was *that* bad."

"Back up, how did you know I got concussed?" Kaiya said, taking a small step back from Briar.

"Do you want me to tell you the truth or not?" Blair remarked, raising an eyebrow. "I could just go home. I don't *need* to be here."

Kaiya moved to say something, some snide remark or another but paused mid-thought. She leaned back against the Ash tree and crossed her arms, mirroring Blair.

"Fine," Kaiya managed as nonchalantly as possible. "Go on."

"Well. Clearly, you don't remember, but you, me, and Opal were all really good friends before she disappeared. My parents and I moved here from Georgia in 2014. Opal had invited me to sit with you two for lunch one day, and from then on, we were inseparable."

Inseparable…? Why can't I remember that?

"*That* day," Blair continued, wincing slightly at the memory, "June twenty-six, 2015, I had caught wind that you two had gone down to the beach to watch the moon. Without me."

Kaiya remained silent, her eyes widening at Briar, urging her to continue.

"So, I had followed you two. I saw where you entered the cave system and found you guys having a picnic inside. I was so upset that I yelled at you both and stormed out. The next morning, I went to apologize, and I found out that Opal had disappeared and you were severely concussed."

"After I told my parents the situation, they immediately took me out of school and transferred me to a private one. Instead of facing you and the Whites, they ran away, taking me with them."

Kaiya nodded, eyeing Briar with a mental magnifying glass.

"Why are you at Atlantic then? You said you were transferred to some private school."

"I was," Blair started, "but because of the mandate, my old school lost almost all of their funding because people rushed to move out. So, I'm at least going to graduate before I move. If this whole moon crap blows over, I was hoping to go to college and get a degree." Blair smiled, just a small one, and met Kaiya's eyes.

Blair looked away.

"Anyways, uhm," Blair said, talking towards the ground, "That's most of it. I know just as much about Opal's disappearance as you do. But you have to know that it wasn't my fault. That's why I didn't talk to you sooner." Blair looked back up, but only with her eyes, a few of her twist-outs falling in front of her lashes.

"So… you've just been avoiding me this whole time because you thought that *I* thought you had something to do with Opal's disappearance?" Kaiya replied sardonically, her eyebrows raised and eyes wide. She threw her hands out to the sides as if to say, *"What the hell?"*

"Well, when you put it like that, it sounds silly—"

"Of *course* it sounds silly! Avoiding me would only solidify my suspicions about you!" Kaiya yelled, her cheeks flushed from the act of exasperation.

"Hush!" Briar rushed over to Kaiya, effectively pinning her shoulders against the Ash tree and putting a finger over Kaiya's lips.

"Look. In hindsight, I can understand why you're upset," Briar said, her head leaning in towards Kaiya, inches apart. Kaiya rolled her eyes and puffed through her nose, but she remained quiet, Briar's finger still on her lips. "If you're ever going to find Opal, you'll need me on your side."

Briar tilted her head to the side, her eyes wide and dewey? As if she were about to cry.

"You lost one friend that day," Briar paused, staring into Kaiya's dark eyes, their intensity trained back into Briar's honey eyes.

"I lost two."

Kaiya's eyelids eased, fluttering shut at the pain she could feel rolling off of Briar. Her dismay spilled over her edges, pouring into the damp forest atmosphere, seeping into the ground. The very earth sighed with Briar.

Much to Briar's surprise, Kaiya's arms wrapped around Briar's waist, pulling her head into the nook of Kaiya's shoulder.

In their embrace, memories flooded back through Kaiya's mind's eye. Playgrounds and beach days and sandcastles whirled past her eyelids, once black, now exploding with colorful nostalgia. The back of Kaiya's head ebbed and throbbed, but not in a painful way. More like the way a stream presses against a dam before the dam bursts, the water finally flowing freely towards the truth.

The trio always slept over together, their sleeping bags pressed together under the shining light of the stars. Briar would bring lunchboxes of food her mom had cooked, straight from a family cookbook. During the winter, when everything was dusted in white, the girls built igloos and snow forts to giggle in, their whispered secrets only melting away with the spring.

In school, at Atlantic Middle, their teachers would pair them together in seating charts, knowing that splitting them up would cause doomsday. Oh, and how they had talked and talked and *talked* for hours, their voices simmering down to whispers only after a day filled with screaming song lyrics and games of pretend. Crashing waves and the restless music of the night weren't even able to drown out their hearts, bleeding onto one another as they spilled their secrets amongst the blankets and constellations.

"Briar…" Kaiya started, her eyes closed and head resting on top of Briar's, their arms still wrapped around each other.

"I'm so sorry. You shouldn't have had to deal with this alone."

"Neither should you, Kay. But we're here, now." Briar replied, a little muffled, her face still buried in Kaiya's shoulder. "Together."

The light rain slowed into a mist, the air growing warmer again, the clouds shifting over the horizon. Above the roof of the Ash trees, the bright blue sky peered down on the reunion of two friends, embraced like the ocean upon the shore.

IX.

Considering the geology unit test was tomorrow, June first, Kaiya assumed that she would be able to identify what the hell happened to the rocky floor of the Atrium, especially with a second pair of eyes.

That is, if she were able to get back into the Atrium.

"I haven't been back here in years. It looks… greyer." Blair remarked, carefully watching her feet as she stumbled down the sandy trail from Abbott's Hill to Niboiwi Bay. She wore wide blue jeans with a pink cheetah print top tucked into the waistband, more indicative of her style than the grey sweatsuit she typically wore to school.

"I guess things look a lot brighter when you're a kid. Less sad." Kaiya replied, her eyes looking out past the trees towards the bay.

"Damn, you didn't need to get all existential on me."

Kaiya stopped cold and faced Briar, "Did you just

curse?"

"Damn right I did. LOL." Briar giggled, throwing her hands up in a carefree shrug.

"Did you just seriously say 'LOL' out loud?" Kaiya laughed, literally out loud. Her eyes were set on Briar, sunlight streaming behind her twists like a halo. Briar's cheeks squished up in a smile, lines creasing the outsides of her eyes, liquid gold.

God, puberty hit her like a truck.

Kaiya blinked a few times, realizing her eyes were particularly dry. She shook away her thoughts and turned back towards the trail when a bright flash of color caught her eye.

Briar resumed her treacherous descent down the sandy trail, saying, "You know, when you said you wanted me to see something back in the sea cave, I never expected that the trail would be this-"

"*Shh.* Look." Kaiya cut her off, putting her left arm out to stop Briar's advancements. Once Briar was on equal footing with Kaiya, safely tucked behind a tree, she nodded down the trail, indicating where she wanted Briar to look.

Yellow tape crisscrossed the end of the trail just before it opened up to the beach. CAUTION: DO NOT CROSS was written in blinding letters across the tape. A police car was parked in the sand, MAINE NATIONAL GUARD was written across the side of the SUV. Three white officers were talking and hanging around the hood, not yet noticing Kaiya and Briar further up the trail.

"What the hell?" Briar whispered harshly, grabbing Kaiya's arm for stability.

"I don't know! They weren't there a few days ago!"

Kaiya exclaimed, just a smidge too loudly.

The officers paused and looked up towards where Kaiya and Briar were crouched. One of the men put his hand on his pistol, not yet drawing it out.

"Hello? Who's up there?" A gruff man with a beer belly called out, seeming to be the oldest of the officers, his long beard greying.

Briar and Kaiya looked at each other, terror in their eyes. Briar was the first to put her hands high in the air and slowly step out into the sight of the officers. Kaiya quickly followed suit, her hands in the air, fully visible to the cops.

Remember, Kaiya. Mrs. Abbott's voice cooed from her subconscious, a long-forgotten memory. *Always be wary of the police, even if you know you have done nothing wrong. They have always feared the people they could never understand.*

"We just wanted to get down to the beach." Briar stuttered out, a forced smile on her lips, her hands still raised. Her knees shook ever so slightly, even though the ground she stood on was flat.

The three cops looked at each other, side-eyeing the girls as they whispered to each other. The one officer took his hand off of his gun, his hand snaking into his pocket.

"The beach is closed until further notice. Governor Harvey's orders." The eldest cop barked, his arms crossed over his broad chest, just above his protruding gut.

Kaiya turned towards Briar, her eyes saying, "What do you *mean* we can't go down there?" Her eyes darted around the landscape. The forest floor outside of the trial was littered with leaves from the previous fall, a brown trench of god knows what. Further down the beach, where one of the public docks was, another cop car was parked, its lights flashing blue and red.

Briar's eyes widened back at Kaiya, an obvious warning to make sure she didn't do anything stupid.

They have guns.

"*Hey!*" The third officer roared towards Kaiya, noticing her glances around the forest. "Don't you go messing around trying to get down here, young lady. We have full authority to arrest you if you try to make it down by the water."

"Yessir. Of course, sir, we'll be on our way." Briar yelped, scrambling to turn around and head back up the trail. She grabbed Kaiya's wrist with an inhuman force, practically dragging her back up Abbott's Hill.

"What the *hell*, Briar? We need to get back to the Atrium! I had everything under control!" Kaiya whispered harshly, Briar leading the two roughly up the path, not looking back to face Kaiya. Briar's acrylic nails, baby pink, dug into Kaiya's skin.

"Kaiya, we could have been *shot*! And you're worried about a stupid sea cave?" Briar seethed; a silk ribbon that tied back part of her twists bounced as she muscled up the rocky trail.

"Let go of me," Kaiya growled, leaning back against the force of Briar's hand on her wrist, Briar's grip like iron.

"No, Kay. I'm not letting you go back there," Briar yanked, physically dragging Kaiya forward.

Goddamn, she's stronger than she looks.

"Briar, let me *go*!"

"*NO!*" Briar whipped around, letting go of Kaiya's wrist, and grabbed Kaiya's face with both of her hands, their eyes mere inches apart. Kaiya's chest rose and fell rapidly, her eyes darting around Briar's face. Fear, anger, and something else lingering in the recesses of her golden eyes. Beads of sweat started to accumulate on Briar's dark skin.

"You would have been *shot* if you tried to go down there. Those were *National Guardsmen*," Briar practically yelled, shaking Kaiya's head with her hands. "God, I just wish you wouldn't be so, so reckless!"

Kaiya could feel the hot impact of Briar's words on her skin, burning brighter than her desire to reach the Atrium. Briar's hands still cupped the sides of Kaiya's face, trapped in an immovable grip, yet Kaiya made no move to break the contact.

Briar's face relaxed, her eyes filling up with tears, which she poorly masked from Kaiya. Her pupils were huge, her honey irises reduced to a thin border between the whites of her eyes and her pupils.

"*I can't lose you again*," Briar whimpered, a tear falling down her cheek as she leaned her forehead against Kaiya's. The two girls closed their eyes, their breathing eventually evening out into a natural rhythm of exhalation.

"Briar... I'm so sorry. I didn't mean to scare you. I just... we just need to get back to the Atrium. I'm closer now than I ever have been to figuring out what happened to Opal." Kaiya whispered as she wrapped her hands around Briar's wrists, pulling the two closer together. Briar sighed and nodded, her weight shifting more towards Kaiya.

"C'mon. Let's get you home." Kaiya murmured into Briar's ear, rubbing her shoulders comfortingly until Briar's hands fell back to her sides. The two girls started their trek back up to the Abbott's house, where Briar's car was parked in front of. Around them, the Ash tree branches swayed in the ocean breeze, the moon watching over their ascent from her place on the horizon.

.ₑↄ§Cₑ.

Briar waved from the front seat of her army green Subaru Forester as she pulled out of the Abbott's driveway. Kaiya waved back, watching her drive away from the safety of the stone pathway that led up to the front door. Even after Briar's car had driven out of sight, Kaiya lingered outside her house, the damp summer air filling her lungs. Darkness seemed to creep in from the surrounding wood, only to be held off by the glass light fixture next to the Abbott's front door. The new moon hung amongst the stars, a dark sphere that blocked out a great deal of the sky. Ash trees of varying heights swayed in the ocean breeze, their branches reaching out towards each other.

A particularly strong gust of wind caused Kaiya to wrap her arms around herself, goosebumps pimpling her skin. She walked up the stone pathway towards the front door, glancing down the driveway one last time before jostling the handle open with her foot.

Compared to the dim lighting of the glass fixture outside, the house was unbearably bright. Kaiya pushed the door shut with her hip, the wood squeaking as it closed. Music streamed through the halls, a soft piano melody that seemed vaguely familiar, an echo of something long since played.

No one has touched our piano in years…

After silently slipping off her shoes, Kaiya tiptoed through the entry hallway. Her footsteps gently padded against the hardwood floor of the kitchen. Once past the granite island that housed the oven, Kaiya reached the doorway that led into the parlor room. She seldom ever went into that room of the house, considering the door was typically closed. Once a room of social gatherings, centered around a grand maple piano, now reduced to a secluded office space for Mr. Abbott.

Kaiya's back was pressed against the wall next to the door's trim. The white paneled door hung ajar on its hinges, a rare occurrence. Now that she was closer, Kaiya could identify the tune.

Somewhere over the rainbow, way up high.

Completely enveloped by the melody, Kaiya closed her eyes as memories of playing the piano pushed to the surface of her mind's eye.

And the dreams that you dream of, once in a lullaby.

Hours upon hours of afternoons and evenings had been spent on that maple stool, little legs barely reaching the pedals. She would start playing while the sun was high in the sky and wouldn't cease until long after the sun had set. Mr. Abbott's large hands would glide over the keys, showing his daughter which notes to play effortlessly. Mrs. Abbott would sit on an embroidered cushion stool, a delicate ukulele in hand, and strum along with her husband, singing a soprano counterpart to her lover's baritone.

Somewhere over the rainbow, bluebirds fly.
And the dreams that you dream of, dreams really do come true.
Now, however, the pace of the song was slower,

less lighthearted. There was a pause before each note, each lyric, silences filling in the gaps of the music. Kaiya pictured her father sitting behind the piano on the maple stool, his eyes closed as his hands flew across the keys. She dared not lean into the doorway for fear of interrupting the song.

A light touch on Kaiya's arm jolted her from her reminiscing. Her eyes shot open, Mrs. Abbott in front of her with her finger on her lips.

"Shhh. Don't make it stop," Mrs. Abbott's eyes seemed to say, hushing any sounds from Kaiya. She waved her hand and pointed upstairs, ushering her daughter to follow. The pair padded quietly through the kitchen, their steps a soft cadence on the dark hardwood. They snuck through the kitchen and past the living room, the black screen of the television reflecting the two women. Mrs. Abbott crept up the staircase first, her body grazing the wall as she went, not a squeak emanating from her steps. Kaiya followed, not as familiar with the path of least sound, a creak or two resounding from her tiptoed pace.

Mrs. Abbott paused at the top of the stairs, looking down on her daughter. She motioned her head towards Kaiya's bedroom and ambled inside without another backward glance, the door already hanging open. Kaiya followed, quietly closing the door behind her. The piano music persisted through the closed door, muted and dull. Mrs. Abbott stood a few feet inside the room, rocking back and forth on her heels.

"Is that who I thought it was?" Mrs. Abbott grabbed Kaiya's forearms and whispered harshly, even though the door to Kaiya's room was sealed shut.

"Huh? What are you talking about?" Kaiya responded, her thoughts flurrying through her head as to what new disappointing action had caused her Mother's displeasure.

"The girl. Blair. That's who you just went out with, wasn't it?" Mrs. Abbott seethed, knocking her head towards Kaiya's window, which looked out over Niboiwi Beach.

Oh, crap!

"What? No, no, that was, um, Bo. She's a new girl in class," Kaiya stuttered out, eyes wide.

What does she have against Briar?

"You take me for a fool, Kaiya Mitena. Bo was just a nickname for Blair Otieno, her initials," Mrs. Abbott paused for a breath, her eyebrows furrowed together in vexation. "You were never meant to see her again. She's trouble."

"*What?*" Kaiya shot back. "What do you mean, 'she's trouble?' She had to go through the same thing I did!"

"Which is the exact reason why you can't be around her!" Mrs. Abbott's voice was hoarse and strained as she attempted to keep her voice down.

"Mother, I can't believe—"

"*I can't lose you, too!*" Mrs. Abbott bawled, grabbing Kaiya's shoulders with her hands and shaking her daughter as tears welled up in her eyes. Downstairs, the soft piano music stopped.

Bewilderment sketched across Kaiya's face as she leaned away from Mrs. Abbott's grasp.

Who is this woman, and what has she done with my mother?

Mrs. Abbott pulled Kaiya into her arms, sobbing

into Kaiya's thick black hair. Kaiya slowly wrapped her arms around her mother, apprehensively patting her back.

There, there?

Behind the duo, the bedroom door opened roughly, the metal handle swinging back into the drywall with a *crack*.

"What is going on in here? Kaiya, what did you say to your mother?" Mr. Abbott barked, his stare burning into Kaiya's back. She pulled away from her mother's teary embrace to face her father. Just as she was about to answer, Mrs. Abbott responded from behind Kaiya.

"It's about Briar." Mrs. Abbott sniffed, her voice wavering.

"I know, Winona." Mr. Abbott's face went stone cold. He stalked over to the bed where his wife and daughter sat, towering over them. He reached out his hands to comfort his wife, rubbing her shoulders as she tried to quiet her sniffling.

"We've been more than accommodating for your recovery process," Mr. Abbott said, looking down at Mrs. Abbott. "We let you search the caves even as the moon situation got worse. We let you grieve in whatever way you needed to."

Kaiya scooched back against the footboard, sensing an outburst.

"And now?" Mr. Abbott finally met Kaiya's eyes. "You decide to go galavanting with Briar of all people? The last time you saw that girl, Opal disappeared." He seethed, the calm piano man washed away.

"We're just trying to keep you safe, honey." Mrs. Abbott cut in, deflecting the severity of Mr. Abbott's statement. Her eyes had mostly dried, though they still remained red and puffy.

"Briar had nothing to do with Opal's disappearance! If anything, she's trying to help me find her, which is more than either of you can say!" Kaiya burst out, her eyes wide, mouth hanging slightly ajar.

"You're not ever going to find Opal! She's gone, Kaiya, and you need to accept that and move on." Mr. Abbott spat back, raising his voice. He leaned over his wife to get closer to Kaiya, his eyebrows scrunched together.

"We've only wanted to help you heal, honey-" Mrs. Abbott started, leaning in to try and separate Mr. Abbott and Kaiya.

"I don't care about *healing*! All I've ever wanted was for you to *support me*! All you've ever done is make me feel like a stranger in my own house!" Kaiya screamed, her parents taken aback by the sudden outburst of noise. She put her head into her palms, realizing the warm wetness on her hands was her tears.

For a moment, there was silence. Aching, drawn-out, stale silence that threatened to choke those stuck in it. No one breathed, just silent tears and wordless glances.

The sound of shuffling cloth broke the quiet, piercing the bedroom like a gunshot. Arms wrapped around Kaiya's curled-up form, shifting her towards the center of the bed. She could have protested. Could have.

One pair of arms enveloped Kaiya's body, her head on their chest, the heartbeat thumping against her ear. Kaiya turned her head and looked up, her teary eyes seeming to deceive her.

Mr. Abbott was cradling his daughter, tears racing

101

down his cheeks. Up close, Kaiya noticed a five-o'clock shadow on his chin, not cleanly shaven. His strong arms tightened around his daughter, not seeming to let go any time in the near future. Beside him, Mrs. Abbott leaned against his shoulder. She reached out to grab Kaiya's hand, which she took without protest.

The three stayed there, silent but collective in their understanding of their own personal worlds, now crashed into one another. A mother, a father, and their daughter embraced in a collision of perspectives, now able to understand the other one's sight.

Kaiya sniffed, breaking the quiet atmosphere. Mrs. Abbott let out a labored sigh, leaning further into her husband.

"I'm so... so sorry." Mr. Abbott managed to whisper, his normally stern voice shaking. "I only ever wanted you to be safe and careful."

Kaiya nodded into her father's chest, not able to bring her throat to say something in return.

So this... this is how they processed their grief.
All while I pushed them away during mine.

The family stayed there until sleep whisked them away to their dreamlands. And yes, *family* does seem to be the appropriate term to describe the Abbotts, however roundabout that term came to be.

X.

The last two weeks of Kaiya's high school experience culminated in many movies and outdoor lunch periods spent with Briar. Everyone in Atlantic High School's senior class was busy planning out trips inland and detailing college plans. Mr. White's geology test had gone well enough that Kaiya had managed to pass his class with a ninety-five percent for the year, the highest out of all of her classes.

However laborious it may seem, studying does pay off, kids.

Now, bright baby blue skies stretched across the horizon, not a cloud in sight to shade from the high June thirteenth summer sun. The forest of Ash trees surrounding the Atlantic High School football field swayed with the ocean breeze, their mighty boughs full once again with leaves. The quiet sound of distance waves crashed against a cliffside if one paid enough attention to hear them.

Black folding chairs were laid out across the turf

in neat, evenly spaced rows. A name tag with a list of achievements adorned the backs of each seat, the leather already warm by the light of the June sun. The bleachers were filled to the brim with people; siblings, parents, grandparents, cousins, and friends all tightly pressed against each other, waiting. Upbeat music played from the stadium loudspeakers, the songs crackling in and out of reception from satellite interference.

Get it? Because the moon is Earth's satellite?

Behind a red brick building where the concession stand was held, the senior class of 2020 of Atlantic High School waited in an alphabetized single file line. Their black caps and gowns rustled in the wind, their voices murmuring nothings into the humid summer air. These children, young adults more like, stood hidden from the view of the families and friends that raised them.

I can't believe this is finally happening...

Kaiya glanced around at her fellow peers. Their faces had changed so much in the past four years, growing into young adults about to be thrust into the vast, doomed world. Once innocent and naive, now mature and wise.

Or at least more mature and wiser than when they were tiny Freshmen.

Now, standing amongst the pupils she had grown alongside, Kaiya couldn't help but think about what today would have looked like if *she* had been here. Her silky blonde hair would have flowed out the sides of her graduation cap, a permanent smile plastered on her cheeks. She would say, "*Kay! Look how far we've come! We've made it!*"

Kaiya closed her eyes, her face towards the sun. Its light burned against her cheeks, a warm kiss from the burning star. She breathed in, her exhale releasing more than just air. Anxiety and reluctance flowed from her lips, her chest relaxing as the weight was lifted from her body, if only temporarily.

I can't cry. Not today. If I cry, that means... that means it's really over.

It's not over.

I'm not finished yet.

Kaiya opened her eyes again. *Abbott* was the first last name of her class, so there she stood. First in line, the lead. Solitarily while her classmates were meant to follow.

When she turned around, one last look back on her past, her peers she would be leaving behind, one face stood out to her. How could it not?

Briar Otieno.

Kaiya sighed, tilting her head to the side, her dark eyebrows scrunched up, a smile turning up her lips. Briar smiled back, the kind of grin you do when you're trying not to cry, lips quivering, a frown morphing into a small smile of joyous melancholy.

Behind Kaiya, a whistle blew. One of the gym teachers, the class of 2020's sponsor, had blown her whistle to get the attention of the seniors. Kaiya whipped around at the sharp noise and met the gym teacher's eyes.

"Time to go."

A few strands of Kaiya's dark hair fell into her face as she turned back towards Briar, their eyes meeting across the distance. "*It's okay. I'm right behind you,*" her eyes seemed to say, nodding as she ushered Kaiya forward.

Light piano music replaced the grainy pop song that streamed from the old stadium speakers. Every member of the audience took to their feet, applauding at the sight of the line of seniors. The soon-to-be graduates walked along the turf, following the furthermost painted white line that denoted the edge of the football field.

Kaiya waved, her eyes scanning over the sea of spectators. Their faces all seemed to morph into one another, their features blurred by the hands of the wind, dull strokes washed out by the sunrays.

How long is this freakin' football field?

Kaiya continued down the painted line, still searching for her parents amidst the crowd. She could hear the rustling of the many gowns that trailed behind her, cheap silk against colored rope cords and satin sashes.

My arm hurts.

The first row of chairs was only ten yards away, and Kaiya still hadn't spotted her parents. Kaiya's waving slowed to a more leisurely gesture, her body now running on autopilot.

I should've brought sunglasses.

As she was about to turn the corner towards her row, Kaiya's foot caught on a loose lump of turf, a short stumble that was sure to be on everyone's videocameras. She turned quickly down her row, speeding toward her seat so she could sit down. At least her graduation cap provided some shelter from the hundreds of eyes that bore through her, laughing and snickering.

Well... At least my parents didn't see that.

The minutes that followed crept by, agonizingly slow, as the rest of the senior class took their seats in their respective rows. Spectators hollered and whistled, feeling more like a sports game than high school graduation. Dr.

Dyche, the principal of Atlantic High School, emerged from the steps of stage right after the last student had sat down.

Dr. Dyche, dressed in the school's colors, blue and grey, sauntered over to a podium in the center of the stage, the Atlantic High School crest carved into its wooden surface. There must have once been paint on the emblem, but it had since dulled and flaked off. She tapped the microphone on the podium with her index finger, the speakers pounding from the sound. The audience sat down once more, the stadium quieting until there was only the rustling of the trees.

"Good afternoon, Atlantic High! My name is Dr. Dyche, the principal of this wonderful school. I would like to thank you all for coming out today to support our graduating class of 2020!" The crowd burst into applause at Dr. Dyche's introduction.

"Now, before we hand out everyone's diplomas, please give a warm welcome to the Atlantic High School class of 2020's valedictorian, Olivia Whiles!" Dr. Dyche said, outstretching her arm out above the podium to wave over the next speaker.

A blonde girl, Olivia, stood up from the very last row, right behind Briar. She walked with fervor, but not in an anxiety-ridden way. Her strides were long and consistent, purposeful. A young woman on a mission. The crowd of spectators resumed their applause, a couple on their feet and whistling. Olivia's parents, no doubt.

Kaiya turned her head back towards the families, wanting one last cursory look around the stadium for her parents. After the valedictorian and teacher representative speeches, Kaiya would be up.

C'mon... please.

Olivia Whiles cleared her throat, bringing Kaiya's attention back up to the stage. The audience went silent once more, waiting for the valedictorian to speak.

"I would like to thank you all for coming here today to celebrate the accomplishments and future endeavors of my fellow students. The past four years have been a whirlwind of memories. Crying, laughing, screaming, more crying," the crowd laughed, a natural reaction to Olivia's sweet, melodic voice. Once the laughter died down, Olivia continued.

"We've grown up, probably much faster than we should have. When we were younger, all we ever wanted was to grow up and get jobs. Live on our own. Now... I'm not so sure about you guys, but I wish that I hadn't taken that time for granted."

Kaiya looked down from the podium, her eyes examining her hands in her lap. She started to turn back towards her peers, maybe catch a certain someone's eye, but thought better of it. Better not draw any more attention to herself than necessary.

"Do you remember playing basketball after school with some guys, even though you've never played basketball before?" Olivia continued, "Do you remember sitting outside for lunch, eating the crappy school food that was a little too questionable?" Chuckles rippled through the senior class. "Don't you remember passing by your friends in the halls, waving, smiling, maybe even stopping for a hug? Look around at all of these shining faces around you. Do you recognize them? Are they the same people who walked through those double doors four years ago?" The valedictorian paused for a second, the question sinking into her peers.

"No. Nothing is the same as it once was. Does that change make us liars? Villains of adaptation? Again, no."

"Amidst battles of academic valor, sports competitions, and an impending lunar apocalypse, heroes were born," Olivia gestured out towards her peers. "You don't wear capes or super suits, but you all have made it *so* far. No one, *no one,* can ever take that away from you. So, when you walk off of this field, diploma in hand, and you stand in front of the great door of your future, don't cower before its immensity. Knock that door off of its hinges and seize your future because not even the *moon* can take it from you!" Olivia shouted the last sentence, throwing her fist up into the air as the other seniors cheered, rising to their feet.

Dr. Dyche waltzed back up to the podium, giving Olivia a quick hug and a pat on the back. The valedictorian turned on her heel with a smile and started back towards her seat in the last row. Dr. Dyche straightened out her pantsuit jacket with a flick of her wrists as she situated herself back on the podium.

"Ladies and gentlemen, another round of applause for Atlantic High School's valedictorian, Olivia Whiles!" Dr. Dyche gestured back towards Olivia as she strutted back to her seat, waving and smiling as she went. The crowd erupted into applause, the students clapping and whooping, the stadium a complete cacophony of noise.

Kaiya clapped lightly, her hands calloused and raw in places from moving boxes and furniture. Her eyes were towards the stage but not quite focused on the principal.

Behind the stage, looming over the Niboiwi horizon, the moon watched over the ceremony. Her craters could house entire Ash trees, roots and all. The bright summer sun's rays bounced off of the moon's surface in a silvery glow. A momentous backdrop for a doomed senior class.

Dr. Dyche used her hands to quiet the crowd, waving up and down until silence reigned over the field. There was some shuffling behind the stage, the curtains rippling from velvet handprints.

"And now, as decided by the students of Atlantic High, I present to you the Class of 2020's teacher representative, Mr. White! Let's give him a hand, shall we?" The principal waved over the biology teacher as she stepped to the side of the wooden podium. Mr. White, clad in a navy button-down and grey slacks, shuffled onto the stage from behind the side curtains. He nodded toward Dr. Dyche, took a deep breath, and took to the podium. As he straightened his clip-on tie, his gaze met Kaiya's.

She looked back at her hands, shaking, picking at the chipped white nail polish her mother had forced her to wear.

"Ehem," Mr. White cleared his throat, the sound echoing through the stadium speakers. "Hello, there, students and families of Atlantic High School. As our fantastic principal said, my name is Mr. Arthur White. While I am well aware that I've not had the chance to teach every single one of you seated before me, I am nonetheless grateful for the opportunity to represent your class here today."

Kaiya's eyes remained downward, her eyes wide in order to dry out the tears that threatened to cascade through her mascara. Even without looking, Kaiya could tell that Mr. White was trembling. His voice alone told the tale of his nervousness.

"Four years is quite some time, especially for someone who's only lived a total of eighteen. That's twenty-two percent of your lives that you've spent within the walls of Atlantic High," Mr. White sniffed, the wind blowing slight feedback into the microphone.

"These four years have presented momentous challenges. Be it gravity, the tides, weird animal behaviors, or just simply managing a passing grade. Four years of adjusting, perseverance, and strength." Mr. White paused, his breath catching at the last word."

"Five years ago, I lost my daughter, Opal."

Kaiya's head whipped up to see Mr. White staring at her with cloudy eyes.

She's not gone!

"She would have been sitting amongst you all today," the biology teacher's piercingly melancholic gaze remained on Kaiya. He closed his eyes, a single tear running down his cheek.

"Atlantic High's Class of 2020, if I can impart any sense of wisdom unto you, let it be this," Mr. White's voice wavered slightly, a thick Ash tree standing stoic against the harsh winds of grief. Kaiya's eyes never left Mr. White's.

"Don't be afraid to live your life. At the end of the day, you are the only one living it. You never know which day will be your last. Once you walk off of this stage, diploma in hand, go out and *live*. Truly, authentically, and freely. Your future self will thank you for it." Mr. White exclaimed, his breathing heavy as he waved the crowd goodbye and stepped away from the podium.

All at once, the students around her jumped up from their seats. Some shouted out nicknames and encouragement towards their favorite teacher, their calls piercing through the unanimous applause. Kaiya broke eye contact with Mr. White's receding figure, which eventually disappeared behind the makeshift stage's curtain. She stood up along with her peers, clapping absentmindedly. Best not to stand out, after all.

Kaiya stole a glance behind her, the tassel of her graduation cap swinging as her head turned. Briar's golden irises met her mahogany ones, the two locking eyes, their cheeks damp with salty tears. The ocean breeze swelled in tandem with the applause, nature's woodwind symphony a song of longing between the Earth and the sea.

A sharp knock on the microphone broke Kaiya's gaze as her peers' heads bobbed back down into their seats. The applause subsided, bringing Kaiya's attention back to Dr. Dyche. Spare strands of brown hair blew against her temples, the gale attempting to unwind her top-knot bun.

"Now, without further ado, let's gift our seniors their hard-earned diplomas!" Dr. Dyche exclaimed into the microphone, shuffling around some papers. Another administrator, a shorter man with balding hair, stood in between Dr. Dyche and a table stacked full of leather-clad diplomas, ready to hand over the awards in an assembly line.

Goddamn... this isn't real.
It's not happening.

Kaiya's palms were drenched in sweat, and not from the summer sun. She clamped her eyes shut, trying to calm her breathing.

In… two, three. Hold.

Hold, Kay.

Out… two, three.

"First up, Kaiya Abbott!" Dr. Dyche declared, lifting her arm out, waving Kaiya up towards the stage.

Just like rehearsal. Just don't trip. Just walk forward, take the paper, and leave.

Kaiya pressed her hands against her knees, using her arms to stand up. Her white platforms wobbled slightly on the uneven turf, Kaiya's knobbly knees not making matters better. She kept her head down as she shuffled towards the stage stairs.

Didn't the construction class kids do this? Is this even safe to stand on?

The platforms landed on the plank stairs with a dull thud, one foot in front of the other. The thirty seconds it had taken Kaiya to cross the distance from her chair to the stage had dragged on for an eternity. Her blood pumped in her ears, completely overbearing the applause of the crowd.

If they're even clapping. They don't know who I am. Why should they clap?

Kaiya finally looked up, meeting Dr. Dyche's eyes. She reached out with her right hand, grasping Kaiya's hand firmly as she handed over the diploma with her left hand.

"Smile for the camera." Dr. Dyche whispered through smiling teeth, nodding her head towards a woman hidden behind a camera, crouched next to the exit stairs.

Diploma in one hand, her other sweaty palm locked with her principal's, Kaiya turned her shoulders toward the photographer. She smiled, but it didn't quite reach her eyes.

Click!

The bright light of the camera momentarily blinded Kaiya, painting a large black dot across her vision. She teetered toward the exit stairs, just as she had practiced during rehearsal. Dr. Dyche was already calling out the name of the next student as Kaiya carefully stepped down the stairs.

"Kaiya." A harsh voice whispered, familiar.

She spun towards the source of the sound, seeing the photographer emerge from behind her camera.

"Mother?" Kaiya cried, throwing her arms around Mrs. Abbot. If it wasn't clear before, it was surely evident now that a hurricane of tears ravaged Kaiya's face.

"Go find your father. He's standing just inside the fence line." Mrs. Abbott whispered, her smile wide, nodding towards the fence that divided the football field and the stands. She let go of her daughter and resumed the crouched stance with her camera.

Kaiya whirled around to face the fenceline. Mr. Abbott waved to his daughter, his arms outstretched in anticipation of an embrace.

The smile on his lips creased the corners of his eyes.

XI.

It had been a week since Kaiya had seen Briar last. A week since she had gotten her diploma. A week that flew by in a whirlwind of boxes, moving trucks, and commotion. Most of the rooms in the Abbott house had been cleaned out, pictures taken off of the walls, furniture packed away in vehicles that were already transporting their cargo to the Abbotts' new house.

I don't even know where I'm supposed to go from here.
I should've found her by now...

Kaiya sat crisscrossed on the floor of what was previously a guest bedroom. The large metal frame of the king-sized bed had left four small circular imprints on the carpet, the only evidence that anything had been housed in the room. An old vacuum stood lonely in the corner, waiting to be used to clean out the empty room. After close inspection, however, the room's previous purpose came to light.

Years ago, during a time of lighthearted play and worry-less endeavors, this room had been a bright playroom. A floor-to-ceiling window on the far end of the room looked out over the backyard, an old tire swing hanging from a dying branch just inside the backyard's treeline. That window had watched the young girl explore her forested world in the summers. Then, served as protection from the ruthless wintery nights, Kaiya's portal from the warm playroom into Maine's powdery landscape.

The walls had once been a fluorescent yellow mural, a field of sunflowers that Mrs. Abbott had painted while she was pregnant with Kaiya. The field stretched further into Kaiya's imagination than the physical wall ever could have, her mother the painter of her reality, the cones of her retina that colored her world.

In August of 2015, Mrs. Abbott had the room painted a dull grey, burying the mural in a layer of acrylic. The racks of toys and towering dollhouses were sold off to younger families as if their years of inhabiting the playroom were mere seconds. Almost all traces of Kaiya's childhood and… friends from that time were all but wiped away, packaged and sent off to the highest bidder. The only remnants of life before the summer of 2015 existed in pictures and memories locked away in the darkness of the Abbotts' mental basements.

Kaiya sprawled out on the carpet with a slight *thud*, throwing her arms and legs out like a starfish, her eyes towards the ceiling. She exhaled, her lungs collapsing in as she released a breath she didn't realize she had been holding in.

Down the hall, the jingle of a collar and four

footsteps padded towards Kaiya. Blaine bounded into the empty guestroom, pouncing on Kaiya's chest as she tried to sit up.

"Hey, girlie!" Kaiya exclaimed, wracking her fingers through Blaine's puffy coat. Wads of white fur floated off of Blaine as Kaiya pet her, the summer heat a driving force in Blaine's voluptuous shedding.

"I'm alright! I meant to fall, silly." Kaiya laughed in between Blaine's avid licking, covering Kaiya's face in slobber. She tried to roll away from Blaine's relentless kisses, only to smack her head straight into the doorframe.

"*OW!*" Kaiya grunted, her hands flying up to hold the spot where her head had hit the trim. Her legs curled up into her chest as she attempted to rock the pain away.

What is it with me and head injuries?

Kaiya groaned, carefully turning out from her fetal position. She slowly opened her eyes, still rubbing her head, when a strange marking caught her eye.

Near the door, carved into the white wooden trim, almost impossible to see unless one searched for it, was the phrase, *"my little sunflower, grow to the moon."*

Well, that comment didn't age well. Why does everyone have to be so obsessed with the moon all *of the time?*

Kaiya stared at the note, an immortal indication of acknowledgment, forever a part of the house.

A house that she was leaving. For good.

She reached out with one of her hands, grazing the edges of the words. The markings were rough against her fingertips, not at all rounded from the sands of time, as fresh as the day it was carved. No one had touched the message in years.

While Kaiya stared at the message, three rapt knocks resounded from the open door, more a gesture of courtesy than of asking permission.

"Kaiya? Have you finished your vacuuming?" Mr. Abbott said, peering his head around the doorframe. "Why are you on the floor?"

Kaiya scrambled to sit up, not wanting Mr. Abbott to find the subject of her gaze.

"It's... comfy?" Kaiya half-smiled and shrugged, hoping her answer was sufficient enough to divert her father's attention.

"Well, uhm, I was... I was wondering if you were done with your chores or not." Mr. Abbott said, moving fully into the doorway and straightening his spine. He was wearing a burgundy tee shirt, lines creasing the front from being folded up for so long, and a seemingly brand new pair of blue jeans. The only thing missing from his uncharacteristic outfit was a store-bought tag.

"Uhm, yeah, for the most part. I just have to vacuum this room, and then this whole floor is done." Kaiya spluttered, leaning back against her hands. She still wasn't quite used to the whole "I'm your father, but there's an unspoken bond between us now" thing. It was like walking around with a small pebble in your shoe; not exactly painful, but very uncomfortable and needs time before being able to ignore the rock completely.

"Well," Mr. Abbott shifted his weight between his feet, "I was wondering if you wanted to play the piano with me. Since there's already a piano at our new place inland, there's no sense in moving it."

Kaiya blinked a few times, her mouth refusing to

move.

He's... inviting me to do something with him? Willingly? Even after I said I wasn't done with my chores?

"I mean, we don't have to, obviously. I just thought—" Mr. Abbott stammered, grabbing the back of his neck with his hand and looking away.

"I would love to, Dad," Kaiya smiled, a real, genuine grin. Mr. Abbott offered his hand out to his daughter, palm up. He knew full well that she had every ability to get up on her own, but he reached out anyway.

Kaiya took her father's hand, his biceps curling as he pulled her up beside him. Mr. Abbott had done a similar gesture when she was younger, eliciting a muffled giggle of nostalgia as Kaiya straightened up.

Mr. Abbott turned his back to the guest room and started walking down the hall. Kaiya followed, her mind wandering as she padded towards the staircase at the end of the hallway.

Years ago, the hallway had once been covered in crayon markings, primitive cave drawings of neon pink and orange that needed a fresh coat of paint to smooth over. Children's toys had littered the floors, remnants of many games of 'dress up.' The picture frames that had once decorated the hall served as a revolving display of family photos, courtesy of Mrs. Abbott's auto-timer camera sessions. One for each season, four sessions a year. Now, all that remained were nail-shaped holes in the drywall.

Mr. Abbot led Kaiya past her ajar bedroom door, only an inflatable air mattress left inside, and down the staircase into the living room. All the furniture had been packed away into the moving truck, only leaving square peg dents in the carpet. Blaine's collar jingled as she trotted behind the pair.

The trio ambled through the doorway, the wood flooring flowing elegantly from the kitchen to the office. Mr. Abbott's large desk and bookshelf had been taken away already, along with the gray floor rug he kept in the center of the dark hardwood. The grand piano, lid open, sat flushed against the wall that housed the doorway back into the kitchen.

Mr. Abbott pulled out the bench and swung his arm out, nodding for Kaiya to sit. Kaiya knelt into a faux curtsy, a giggle escaping her lips as she sat down on the right side of the stool. Her father followed suit, swinging himself onto the left end of the bench. He smoothed out his jeans with the palms of his hands, an old habit.

Kaiya placed her fingers onto the edge of the piano, leaning forward to stretch until she heard her joints *pop*. She turned towards her father, waiting for his cue to start.

"You ready?" Mr. Abbott chimed, already knowing which duet they were going to play.

"I've always been ready, Dad." Kaiya's lips turned up, curling at the corners, her eyes shining as she readied herself to play.

Mr. Abbott closed his eyes, knowing all too well the notes he needed to play. He started off slow, just the base notes to start. After a few measures, Kaiya's fingers lightly pressed the higher-pitched keys, introducing the melody.

"Oooh, oooh, oooh." Mr. Abbott cooed, his eyes open again, watching the two sets of hands dance across the keys.

"Somewhere, over the rainbow," Kaiya joined in,

Mr. Abbott's baritone voice melding along with Kaiya's soprano vocals. Mr. Abbott's feet controlled the pedals on the floor, the intonation of the keys rising and falling in beautiful crescendoes and decrescendos. The rest of the world melting away as the music reverberated through the air.

"Way up high."

"And the dreams that you dream of, once in a lullaby- hi, hi!" Mr. Abbott's voice strained to reach the higher notes, causing Kaiya to laugh, her fingers stumbling ever so slightly on the ivories. Once she regained her composure, she started the next lyric.

"Someday I'll wish upon a star, wake up where the clouds are far behind,"

"Me-e-e!" Her Dad joined in, nudging his daughter playfully with his shoulder.

"Where trouble melts like a lemon drop, high above the chimney tops," A new voice sang, soprano like Kaiya's, but smoother like aged wine.

The music faltered for a moment, the two pianists looking up towards the new singer. Leaning against the doorframe, Mrs. Abbott stood, nodding for her family to continue the song.

"That's where you'll find me," The Abbotts sang, the air rejoicing at the reunion of song. Mrs. Abbott waltzed over to the piano from the doorway and stood behind her daughter and husband, her hands resting on their shoulders.

"Oh, somewhere over the rainbow,"

"Way up high."

"And the dream that you dare to,"

"Why, oh why, can't I-hi-hi?"

Mr. Abbott stretched out the last syllable, looking up at his wife as he sang. She chuckled, which grew into a burst of head-thrown-back laughter, contagiously spreading to the rest of her family. The tickling of the piano keys faded away, replaced by the organic melodic merriment.

"You've still got it, my little sunflower," Mr. Abbott gushed, winking at the floral nickname. Kaiya pulled her hands back from the piano, her eyes wide in recognition.

The carving in the guest room... wasn't from Mom.

Mr. Abbott smiled as he rested his hands on his jeans, his head tilted to the side as he admired his only daughter. The two looked at each other, an unspoken sense of longing for lost, bitter time sat between them.

"Well," Mrs. Abbott interrupted, finally catching her breath. "I hate to break up this wonderful music, but there are only a few more boxes that need to be brought outside. I wanted you guys to help me out, so we can all pack them away together." Mrs. Abbott's voice started to wavered ever so slightly, her eyes open a little too wide, but the father-daughter duo silently decided not to mention it.

Oh, how the tears were about to pour.

Kaiya and her father stood up from the piano bench and followed Mrs. Abbott back into the kitchen. On the island sat three boxes, all labeled in black scribbled marker, practically illegible. Mrs. Abbott knew what they said, and frankly, that's all that mattered.

Each member of the Abbott family lifted a box from the counter, balancing it between their arms. The door that led directly into the garage from the kitchen was already ajar, the scent of fresh rain flowing in through the doorway.

Kaiya walked out into the garage first, her father and mother trailing behind. The short wooden staircase creaked as she stepped down, the dark hardwood of the kitchen morphing into the concrete floor of the garage.

Normally, buckets of paint would have been stacked on the shelves that lined the garage walls. The Abbotts never parked their family car in here anyways, so Mrs. Abbott was free to use the space as she pleased. Now that all the paint had been packed away, Kaiya could actually see what the color of the wall behind the shelves was.

Gray. Not even a blue-gray or some other fancy color. Just plain, old gray.

Beside the shelves, the garage door had been lifted open. A U-Haul moving truck had been backed in as close to the garage entrance as possible, a means to reduce the time spent moving boxes around in the summery sprinkle. The door to the moving truck was also lifted, revealing a Tetris-style arrangement of other boxes and furniture.

Kaiya lifted her knee up and leaned against the edge of the moving truck. She slid the cardboard box across her thigh until it was securely resting on the wooden planks of the U-haul. Inside, stacks of boxes piled up high, tight to the metal ceiling. A few mattresses were crammed into a narrow crevice along the passenger sidewall. Instead of smelling like home, ginger and lemon tea, the Abbott's earthly possessions took on a must of mildew and salt, the rain fighting to seep through the metal crevices of the truck's roof.

Mr. Abbott came up behind Kaiya, lifting his own box carefully on top of Kaiya's. He grabbed his daughter's shoulder with his hand, pulling Kaiya into a slightly awkward side hug.

He's trying his best, okay?

Mrs. Abbott bumped Mr. Abbott's hip, chuckling lightly as she shoved her own box into the moving truck. After her box was secured, Mrs. Abbott wrapped her arms around her husband and daughter, the light rain anointing their embrace.

"So… that's everything, isn't it?" Kaiya said solemnly, nudging her head into her mother's shoulder.

"Yes, I believe so," Mr. Abbott sighed, his grip loosening slightly.

"I can't believe we're actually leaving," Mrs. Abbott sniffled, a few rebellious tears snaking down her cheeks.

"We'll have each other, and that's really all that matters, right?" Kaiya responded, squeezing her parents tighter at the thought.

"Of course, dear. Of course," Mr. Abbott responded.

The family stayed there in silence, if only for a moment. The light pitter-patter of rain against the sheet metal of the U-Haul ceased, a dull mist replacing the shower.

"Get some rest, my love,' Mrs. Abbott broke the silence as she wiped away her tears. "We leave before the sun rises tomorrow morning."

Mrs. Abbott ushered her daughter with her hands up the stairs of the garage. Mr. Abbott watched from the edge of the garage as their daughter mounted the creaky wooden stairs back into the empty house.

Once Kaiya was safely inside, resting on her blow-up air mattress in her old bedroom, Mr. and Mrs. Abbott closed the door to the U-Haul with a metallic *clang*. The mist had slowed almost completely, the scent of dirt after rain and chirping crickets the only senses to pierce the darkness of the cloudy night sky. Hidden behind the clouds, no doubt, the huge moon loomed, hanging precariously in the balance between heaven and Earth.

XII.

June twenty-sixth, 2020. 4:28 am.

Kaiya Abbott collapsed on the edge of the cliff, her eyes puffy with angry tears, blood streaming down from the cut on her cheek. Around her, the flying debris careened back towards the ground, sharp, flailing projectiles that seemed to circle her crouched form.

The wind entered her lungs without her actually breathing it in. Waves crashed and sprayed salty water on her as the breeze tickled her skin. Every emotion, every moment, every memory of Opal came rushing back to her. Warmth flooded through her veins, straight from her heart, as easy as breathing. It was as if the silence had been suddenly broken by a symphony of piano keys and violin strings, combining into an orchestrated display of nature. Pounding, thumping, Kaiya's heart beat faster than it ever had. It felt like her heartstrings were finally being pulled, how they had ached to be touched. Five long years of cold stone, bitter ice making up her body, melted away like the receding tide.

Kaiya whipped her head up towards the sky, expecting to see the moon's large surface hurtling towards her. Instead, the pre-dawn sky was impossibly dark, only the stars shining in the sheet of black. Where the moon should have been, a silhouette of light floated down from the horizon. Radiant and glowing, with pearly white skin. As the form grew closer, Kaiya's breath caught in her throat even though the winds were slowing down.

Opal?

She was just as tall as Kaiya had remembered, though her features had since filled out with the passage of time, a shining silver toga hugging her curves. The red speckles of acne Opal once wore had healed over into dimpled scars, tiny imperfections, craters. Opal's hair hadn't grown, or at least it didn't seem to have grown, her silky white-blonde curtains just grazing her shoulders. Her eyelashes curled up over her blue eyes, paler and duller than before, like moonlight reflecting off of a pool.

Silver eyeshadow dotted the inside corners of her eyes.

Kaiya's heart crescendoed, a symphony of emotions rising beneath the surface of her skin pushing, pushing for her to reach out. To touch her, to know that she was *there*. Though the wind had stopped almost completely, Kaiya struggled to get air into her lungs. Her throat caught on the image of beauty floating down towards her.

"Opal…?" Kaiya croaked, her voice raw from the screaming and salt, "Is that really you?"

The figure turned her forearms out, her palms

facing the heavens. The silvery toga swayed gently in the air, a bright contrast against the dark horizon. She glided down from the sky, slowly descending until she touched the ground.

Well, her feet never did truly contact the Earth, as she was partially transparent, not fully corporal.

She's still as beautiful as the day she disappeared.

"It's me, Kay," Opal cooed, her voice distant, even though she stood mere inches over from Kaiya.

"I, I can't—" Kaiya stuttered, tripping as she attempted to stand up, the world spinning beneath her feet.

"Woah, woah, okay, I'll sit next to you, okay?" Opal stammered, her voice cracking as she guided her friend back to the ground. She sat next to Kaiya, or at least tried to, her outstretched legs hovering a few centimeters above the grass.

Kaiya's wide eyes never left Opal. Her eyes darted over her friend, the passage of five years evident in her features, but an effervescent shine still gleamed in Opal's eyes. The way that her lips curved up in a grin was the same as before, just as the way she leaned against her palms as if no time had passed. And yet, all the time in the world had been washed away.

Opal smoothed out her toga while looking over Kaiya, her lips slightly parted as if she were about to speak but chose not to. Braces still adorned her pearly white teeth.

"I," Kaiya paused, her eyes blinking shut as she put her head into her hands, her elbows resting on her knees, "What happened, Opal? I've been looking for you for years, and everyone called me crazy, and the video and-"

"I died, Kay," Opal interrupted, two cool pockets of

air cupping Kaiya's hands. "Can you look at me, please?"

Kaiya lifted her head gingerly, slowly opening her eyes. Opal was crouched in front of her, her hands resting on either side of Kaiya's face. Though Kaiya couldn't physically feel the familiar touch of Opal's skin against hers, she could feel the hairs standing up on the backs of her hands, a cold replacement.

Tears streamed down Kaiya's cheeks, her lip quivering and her chest rising and falling rapidly. Her eyes darted around Opal's features, not lingering on a specific part for too long. Opal's silhouette shone lightly, like flashlights on fog, appearing solid yet able to be blown away in a blink.

"You can't be," Kaiya hiccuped and hesitated, "You can't be… gone. That's not how it was supposed to go."

"I know, Kay, I know," Opal sighed, attempting to use her thumb to wipe away Kaiya's tears. Instead, her finger passed right through the drop. Opal pulled her hands away, laced them together in her lap, and frowned. She looked down towards Niboiwi Bay, the waves practically nonexistent. No moon, no tides.

Kaiya tried to calm herself, breathing deeply as she watched Opal gaze off into the sea. Up close, Kaiya noticed that the grey fabric of Opal's toga was rough and speckled with varying grey divots. Shadows of blue scorch marks hide in between the folds. Opal's veins stood out starkly against her pale skin, navy rivers that carried unnecessary cargo.

"What," Kaiya said, just above a whisper, "What happened to you? How are you *here* right now?"

"Well, I remember just as much as you do," Opal

exhaled, looking back at Kaiya through her eyelashes.

"Wait," Kaiya asked, raising her eyebrows. "What do you mean, 'as much as I do?'"

"You might not have seen me in years, Kay," Opal tilted her head to the side, a small smile forming on her lips. "But I've been with you every single day, watching you from up there," She looked up and pointed to the sky in a sweeping motion.

Kaiya only stared at her friend, wide-eyed, the stream of tears slowing to a drip.

"I guess it's best if I just start from the beginning, huh?" Opal straightened up and tucked a strand of hair behind her ear. With a deep breath, she began to speak.

"That night, five years ago, something happened in the cave. I can't remember what exactly happened, but I do remember falling asleep, my heartbeat rapidly falling," Opal hesitated. "Do you remember why we went down to the caves in the first place?"

"Yes," Kaiya nodded, "We were going to see the Supermoon, which is when a full moon is at its closed distance to Earth."

"Look at you," Opal chuckled, her eyes starting to water. "Still smart as ever."

Kaiya let out a single laugh, more an attempt to stave the tears than anything else.

"Just... please don't think I'm crazy."
"Opal?"
"Yeah?"
"I'm talking to the ghost of my best friend—"
"Spirit. Not ghost."
"Okay, *spirit* of my best friend that's been missing

131

for five years," Kaiya remarked, her chest heaving with a laborious exhale. "I would believe *anything* you told me."

Opal hummed affirmatively, her lips trying to smile, trying to be strong.

Strong for Kaiya.

"As I was dying, the Spirit of the Moon, Niboiwi herself, reached down to Earth," Opal paused, searching Kaiya's face for some form of mockery or disbelief. Kaiya simply nodded, hanging on Opal's every word.

Niboiwi isn't just the name of the bay...

"She tried to heal me, but there wasn't anything that could've been done. In the moments before I died, Niboiwi had given me a choice."

"I could either die there, in the Atrium, for you to find me," Opal hesitated, "Or, Niboiwi offered to change me into the moon. I wouldn't be dead, but I wouldn't be able to visit Earth."

"But, I don't understand-" Kaiya began, questions racing through her mind.

"Please, save your questions until I'm finished," Opal whimpered, the tears starting to fall. Kaiya sniffled and nodded, pulling her knees up to her torso.

"I was going to ask to stay on Earth. Then, my parents would've been able to find me, and you could have had a proper goodbye. But," Opal wiped away one of her own tears with the back of her hand.

"When Niboiwi had tried to heal me, she had gotten too close to Earth. Her pull raised the tides, flooding the Atrium with you trapped inside."

"I knew that if I asked her to bring my body back to Earth, you would *drown* trying to save me from the tide." Opal sniffed, her voice catching in her throat as she explained.

She sacrificed herself...so I'd *have a chance to survive.*

"So, I asked Niboiwi to take me with her," Opal cried, burying her face into her palms.

Kaiya wanted more than anything to reach out, to touch, to comfort Opal. She had to make an impossible decision, eye to eye with death. On her own.

Alone.

"Oh my god," Kaiya croaked, staring at Opal's hunched form. "I'm *so* sorry, O. I *never* should have taken you to that damned cave. This... this is all my fault."

"*No*," Opal's head whipped up from her hands, "Don't you dare blame yourself. Just because I'm gone doesn't mean your world has to end too." Her voice shook, momentarily stunning Kaiya at the outburst.

"Kay, you have to move on or else...." Opal trailed off, looking down at her palms in her lap.

"Or else *what*, O?" Kaiya asked, eyebrows raised, "I can't just forget about you. That'd be impossible!"

"Catastrophy, Kaiya!" Opal yelled, throwing her hands out. "Why do you think the moon closed in on Earth?"

"Well, um, the scientists said they think—"

"It was *you*, Kaiya. *You* pulled me back to Earth. Back to you."

The world went quiet, not even the crickets daring to make a sound. Kaiya's jaw dropped, her eyes set into a seemingly permanent wideness. If she thought she had questions before, now she had even fewer answers in the face of a monsoon of queries.

Me? Pull the moon in? That's crazy.
... Right?
That can't be possible.
This isn't real.

Her chest started to rise and fall faster than Kaiya could keep up with, her blood screaming for more oxygen. The cliff started to blur in with the sky, her vision a kaleidoscope of the dark landscape.

"Kaiya! Please breathe!" Opal screamed, rushing over to Kaiya as she wobbled precariously on the cliffside. "In, and out. *Please*, for me, Kay."

In...

Kaiya sucked in a breath and held it for a moment. The world seemed to stabilize, at least for now, the ocean below and the sky above. Most importantly, Opal's eyes were level with hers.

"So..." Kaiya hesitated, still catching her breath. "*I* started doomsday?"

"Well," Opal started tentatively, searching for the right words. "Not intentionally. You see, your mom, Mrs. Abbott? She truly is related to the original Niboiwi Head Chieftess, who was blessed by Niboiwi herself long ago."

It's true....? I thought that was just a bedtime story.

"Because you have some of the Head Chieftess's blood running through your veins and such a strong connection to me," Opal continued, "Your grief acted as a magnet, pulling Niboiwi and me back to you."

"I just..." Kaiya looked into Opal's eyes, trying to find the words to make up for five years of lost time. "I thought I was doing you justice by never giving up on you."

"And you have! Kay, I couldn't have asked for a

better friend. Both you and Briar made my life into a crazy, wild, love-filled adventure, and that is worth more to me than a thousand lifetimes." Opal beamed, her body shining, reflecting literal sunshine.

"One last question," Kaiya asked, "Are you and Niboiwi separate or…?"

"She is a part of me, just as much as I'm a part of her," Opal placed her hands over her heart and looked out over the sky, melting from black into navy, the premature beginnings of sunrise.

"Just as you are a part of me, Kaiya," Opal sighed and smiled, gently rising to her feet.

"Wait, where are you going?" Kaiya pressed, confusion building in her head, blocking her arteries.

"I have to return to the sky. Earth needs Niboiwi back in her rightful place among the stars," Opal gazed up towards the constellations above, her freckles reflecting the map of the cosmos. She started to hover, slowly rising up above the cliffside.

"But there's so much more I want to say—" Kaiya scrambled to her feet, reaching out the try and touch her friend.

"I love you, Kaiya Abbott," Opal whispered into her ear, leaning down as she was lifted back up into the sky. She kissed Kaiya's cheek, a cool touch against the burning of her cut. One minute, Opal was there, her arm reaching out to Kaiya's like God towards Adam.

Kaiya blinked, and Opal's familiar figure was gone, replaced by the distant face of the moon, far beyond the horizon. She fell to her knees, her gaze never straying from the celestial spirit in front of her.

"I love you too, Opal White," Kaiya murmured, her voice overpowered by the resumed crashing of the bay.

Kaiya reached up to touch her face, desperately trying to hold on to the feeling of Opal's lips on her cheek. Her fingers rubbed at her skin, searching for the blunt edge of the cut. The stinging heat had faded away, the skin smooth to the touch.

My cheek is… healed?

Somewhere in the distance, far behind where Kaiya sat, two people called out, their voices coarse and dire.

"Kaiya!" Mr. Abbott cried, his vocal cords raw as he emerged from the treeline. Mrs. Abbott followed directly behind him, the two sprinting across the clearing towards their only daughter.

Kaiya whipped around, quickly wiping her tears away from her cheeks. Once they became in earshot, Kaiya yelled out to her parents, "I'm so sorry! I didn't mean to run, I just, I needed-"

Mr. and Mrs. Abbott skidded to a stop, dropping down to the ground next to Kaiya, enveloping her in their arms.

"Oh my god, Kaiya! Please don't *ever* do anything like that again!" Mrs. Abbott cried, her hands fumbling to keep her daughter as close as possible.

While Mr. Abbott's arms wrapped around his wife and daughter, he glanced around the scene, checking the area for damage. All around them was carnage; broken glass shards of old windows, car doors, and uprooted saplings were strewn across the cliff's edge. Mr. Abbott pulled away, searching Kaiya for any sort of damage.

"Are you alright, Kay?" Mr. Abbott asked, his eyes

darting over her, brows furrowed. "What the hell happened here?"

"I'll tell you just…." Kaiya managed, her voice coarse, "Not now."

Mr. and Mrs. Abbott looked at each other, concern lining their features. Yet, they simply nodded, turning back to their daughter. They attempted to stand, but Kaiya launched toward them, bringing the family back into a harmonious squeeze.

Over the Eastern horizon, the sun pierced the sky, bursting with color over the Atlantic. A new day had broken over Earth and all of her inhabitants, a new chance. The Abbott family remained in their embrace as rainbows of light cascaded down from the heavens, the gentle ebb of Niboiwi Bay splashing down below. Nearby, sunlight reflected off of a gold-lined glass case, drawing attention to the white flower inside.

XIII.

Life in Maine, as well as the rest of Earth, steadily calmed down. The National Guard left the beaches. Moving trucks filled the streets again, people bustling to and fro with boxes and bins in their grasp, unpacking. Few people complained about insomnia, which alleviated many daily headaches. Local news stations covered more miscellaneous stories as the moon's large image slowly receded from everyday vernacular.

A pile of cardboard boxes and haphazardly placed furniture decorated the Abbott's living room. Sure, they could be spending their warm summer day unboxing.

Could be.

Instead, the family sat outside amongst the sand, looking out onto Niboiwi Bay. Blaine bounded back and forth along the edge of the surf, Mr. Abbott's arm a catapult for a worn-out tennis ball. Mrs. Abbott reclined against a built-up pile of sand, an easel mounted into the ground in front of her. She painted what she saw; for once, the scene felt real, tangible. Not abstract.

And Kaiya? She laid down between them atop a red checkered blanket, soaking up the light of the sun, eyes shut, in denim shorts and a gray tee shirt.

Everything really did turn out okay, didn't it?

The rift between the members of the Abbott family had since healed; golden adhesive held together the previous cracks. Now, Abbott Hill felt whole again.

Opal was safe, content and preserved by the moon spirit's grace. She was able to shine her light for the whole world to see, which wouldn't have been possible if she was still on Earth. Kaiya knew she was there in the sky, always watching over her. A celestial guardian angel.

Well, not *just* watching over Kaiya.

"Kay!" A sweet voice called out from behind the family. Kaiya sat up, dusting sand off of her arms as she turned to face the voice, knowing exactly who it was.

"Hey, Briar! I thought you had work today?" Kaiya replied, using her hand to shield her eyes from the bright summer sun.

"I got off early since there weren't a lot of kids who needed tutoring today. I thought I'd find you here." Briar stumbled down the sandy trail, her arms outstretched for balance. She wore a stunning yellow sundress that hung just below her knees, a wide-brimmed orange hat resting atop her two long box braids.

"Hello, Briar. I like the new 'do!" Mrs. Abbott exclaimed as she turned around from her painting.

"Thank you, Mrs. Abbott!" Briar jokingly curtsied as she replied, finally at the family's little picnic area. In a flash of white, Blaine had sprinted up from the shore to greet Briar.

"Oh! Hello, there!" Briar exclaimed, rubbing her hands over Blaine's increasingly shedding coat. Puffs of white hair clumped off of her, floating down to the sand.

"Someone's excited to see you, huh?" Mr. Abbott said, laughing as Blaine left slobbery kisses on Briar's cheeks. Mrs. Abbott joined in her husband's laughter, forming sweet music that flitted amongst the salty sea breeze.

Kaiya scooched over to Blair, gently pushing Blaine off of her chest. The Samoyed rolled onto her back in between the two girls, wagging her tail as she waited to be pet.

The gentle rolling of the waves against the sand replaced the subsiding sounds of laughter. No longer was the tide monstrous and deafening, but now a soft melody to provide ambiance to the family's ears.

"You know," Briar started, her eyes still focused on Blaine, "I was wondering if I could steal you away for a bit. There's something I want you to see." She mindlessly pet the Samoyed, waiting for her friend's response.

"Sure," Kaiya looked up, trying to catch Briar's eye. "Where were you thinking?"\

"You'll know when we get there," Briar replied, finally looking up. Her honey eyes, locked with Kaiya's, seemed to sparkle in the light of the summer sun. She smiled, a half-smile with a wince of pain, like hydrogen peroxide. Necessary to heal, yet burning hot discomfort.

Kaiya broke away from Briar's gaze, looking towards her parents for silent permission. Not that she needed their permission to go out anyways, but it felt cordial to ask.

"Go ahead, hon." Mrs. Abbott said, nodding for Kaiya to get a move on.

"Just be back for dinner, alright? I'm grilling tonight." Mr. Abbott added, winking at his daughter with a smile. "Briar is more than welcome to join us, too if she'd like."

Kaiya whipped back towards Briar, her face lit up in a huge grin.

"I would love that, Mr. Abbott. Thank you." Briar closed her eyes and nodded her head down, a smile still plastered to her cheeks.

"We'll be back soon, okay?" Kaiya promised, jumping up to her feet. She reached her hand out to Briar, which she took with a laugh. With the two on their feet, they turned back towards the trail that led up Abbott Hill.

"Bye!" Mrs. Abbott called out, Blaine trampling around between her and Mr. Abbott. The married couple waved their daughter away, murmuring to each other as the two girls strolled up the rocky trail.

"Do you remember when we were like that?" Mrs. Abbott asked, turning toward her husband.

"Young?" He responded, raising an eyebrow and grinning.

"Oh, hardly. No," Mrs. Abbott replied as she tilted her head to the side, "to be freshly in love."

.ᓚ⊃§ℂᓗ.

Briar led Kaiya up Abbott Hill, looking over her

shoulder every once in a while to make sure Kaiya still trailed close behind her. The air was warm but not humid, thankfully. It wasn't a tough hike, but the high summer sun made certain that the girls felt the heat.

The Abbott House towered into view, about a quarter-mile up the trail. The moving truck was still parked in the driveway, only half unpacked. What was the hurry?

Briar's green Subaru Forrester peeked out between the Ash trees, parked behind the truck. When the two came upon a fork in the trail, Kaiya assumed they'd be taking the right path back up towards her house. To her surprise, Briar took the left path.

"Wait," Kaiya said, stopping in her tracks. "I thought we were driving to this mysterious place that you wanted to show me?"

"Who said anything about driving?" Briar smirked, her citrine-colored sundress rippling as she turned around. She started walking down the path again, glancing back to see if Kaiya would follow.

"This leads to the White's property, Briar. Are you sure you know where you're going?" Kaiya questioned, still stuck in her spot at the fork in the trail, her arms crossed as she looked down at Briar.

"I know where I'm going, Kay, trust me. I've visited here before." Briar answered dolefully. She extended her arm out towards Kaiya with a half-smile, her palm turned towards the sky.

Kaiya hesitated. She looked up the right path, towards her house, and then down the left trail, Briar's dark arm outstretched, waiting to be taken.

Yellow really is her color, huh?

She sighed, uncrossing her arms as she took a step down the left path. Briar smiled and waited for Kaiya to take her hand.

What could go wrong?

Kaiya reached out and grasped Briar's hand. It was soft and warm, not at all like Kaiya's calloused, frigid hands.

I have circulation problems, okay? Don't judge my cold fingers.

Briar burst into a toothy grin at Kaiya's touch, practically emitting sunshine. Kaiya couldn't help but smile back, her mahogany eyes lighting up like wood in a fire.

The pair started off down the trail again, side by side. Every so often, there would be a break in the trees, unveiling Niboiwi Bay's shining blue waves. Bright-colored warblers swooped in and out of the tree branches, their chirping song ringing through the boughs. It was peaceful, quiet in the way that nature is never quiet.

"We're almost there," Briar whispered, giving Kaiya's hand a tight squeeze.

"Why are you whispering?" Kaiya murmured back, leaning in toward her friend as their steps slowed.

"Out of respect," Briar mumbled, barely audible.

Kaiya stopped in her tracks, her eyes glued to the sight at the end of the trail. White iron wrought fence posts lined the perimeter of a small plot of land. English Ivy crawled up the pickets, but not in a way that the area felt unkempt. Nature had aided in the respectful efforts of this manmade memorial.

An ivory headstone stood towards the back of the space, its inscription indecipherable from a distance. A white bouquet of flowers rested in front of the marker.

"C'mon, Kay," Briar sighed, pulling gently on Kaiya's hand to move her forward.

"I can't... I can't do this," Kaiya sniffed, tears already clouding her eyes, breathing in sharp gasps.

Briar tiptoed back towards Kaiya and wrapped her arms around her waist. Kaiya's arms immediately wound around Briar's neck, her face tucked away into the sandy yellow fabric of Briar's sundress. She cried, her chest swelling with the expansion of her lungs against her ribcage, harsh, shuttering heaves for air. A gust of wind off of the ocean poured through the trees, a solemn attempt to drown out a girl's longing cries.

"Can you take a deep breath for me, Kay?" Briar asked softly, taking Kaiya's face in her hands, her fingers wiping away the tears from Kaiya's cheeks.

Kaiya shuttered in a hazy breath, exhaling with a shiver.

"Let's do that again, okay?" Briar joined in this time, inhaling deeply and exhaling alongside Kaiya.

Kaiya nodded at Briar, closing her eyes and holding out her hand. Gently, Briar took Kaiya's hand and guided her down the remaining length of the trail.

The metal gate creaked open with a slight nudge of Briar's hip. She held the gate open with her foot, guiding Kaiya inside by her hand.

"Can you open your eyes, Kaiya?" Briar asked, just above a whisper, rubbing Kaiya's hand with her thumb in a sweeping motion.

Kaiya inhaled slowly, her eyelids fluttering open. She blinked a few times to let her eyes adjust to the bright summer sun. In front of her, Kaiya saw the burial in greater detail. The ivory headstone was curved at the rims, with no sharp edges in sight. On either side of the headstone, emerald vines climbed up the rock's surface, pale, snow-white flowers blooming along in intervals. Swirling borders were carved delicately into the stone, almost mirroring the climbing stems, sand settled in the shallow divots. Kaiya's eyes scanned over the epitaph on the ivory:

> *In loving memory of*
> *Opal Mae White*
> *June 10th, 2002 - June 26th, 2015*
> *We'll see you on the other side of the stars, my dear.*

Tears rolled down Kaiya's flushed cheeks, watering the grass below. A bouquet of honeysuckles tied together with a yellow ribbon, slightly wilted, rested in front of the headstone. Kaiya knelt down on the grass and reached out to touch the flowers. She looked back up at Briar, her eyes wide and shining. After patting through her back jean short pocket, Kaiya pulled out the gold-lined case, Opal's dried white flower pressed in the center. She thumbed over the glass as Briar knelt down at her side.

"I had never really thought about what kind of flower this was," Kaiya hesitated, "It was a gift from Opal, and I guess that's all that really mattered to me," Kaiya murmured, leaning her head onto Briar's shoulder. She passed the case over to Briar, fiddling gently with the honeysuckles' stems with her other hand.

"It doesn't look like a honeysuckle," Briar questioned, tilting her head to the side while holding the glass up to her eyes. "The petals are too wide."

"Wait," Kaiya drew her hands back from the bouquet. "Can I see that again?"

"Of course," Briar handed back the gold case, her eyebrows raised.

Kaiya extended her arm out to its full length, the case sandwiched delicately between her thumb and forefinger. The case was positioned in such a way that the fragile, dried blossom blocked out the headstone, and the trailing plants beside it framed the edges of the glass.

"Oh my god," Briar whispered, not daring to move.

"It's the same flower!" Kaiya exclaimed, throwing her arms up in excitation. A family of warblers took flight from a nearby tree at the sudden outburst of noise.

"There's still the issue of what exactly the flower is," Briar remarked, "It's species, I mean."

"It's a good thing we know someone who knows a thing or two about plants," Kaiya beamed up towards Briar. However, as quickly as the smile came, it fell away.

"That means you'd have to see…." Briar started.

"I know," Kaiya sighed, "It's about time I go, though. I owe it to them."

A quiet descended upon the young women, their eyes locked together. The breeze tickled their skin, and the distant crashing of the bay echoed through the air. Sunshine refracted the colors of Maine into brighter hues, a kaleidoscope filter of dense pigments. The Ash trees waved their verdant limbs towards the effervescent cerulean sky. Rising above the Niboiwi horizon, the pearly surface of the moon shone onto the water. She was only a small portion of the sky now, back to her normal distance of two hundred and thirty-eight thousand, nine hundred miles away. Distant, gazing.

"I'll be back soon," Kaiya stood up, dusting a few

particles of sand from her legs.

"Will you let me know what she says?" Briar questioned, standing up to her full height next to Kaiya.

"Of course," Kaiya leaned in and wrapped her arms around Briar, gold case in hand.

"Be careful, please," Briar whispered, looking down, "For me."

"As you wish," Kaiya said earnestly, tucking one of Briar's boxer braids behind her ear, out of the way of her sunhat.

Briar grinned, the lines around her eyes softening as she watched Kaiya turn and recede down the trial, walking toward a small cottage nestled between Abbott's Hill and the sea.

XIV.

In contrast with the modern architecture of Kaiya's house, the White's home is more like a seaside cottage. Blue sun-streaked paint covered the window shutters that adorned the window panes. The exterior walls were light cream and rough from withstanding the seasonal battering of the coastal winds. The White's home has a large wrap-around porch, complete with an awning, in which three rocking chairs were perched. On their birch front door, a bronze sun-shaped hand knocker stood guard.

Kaiya ambled up the sandy path that her feet had longed to tread again. It had been years since she had visited here, and it certainly showed. As she approached the front door, flowers lining the stone pathway, there came a barking.

They have a dog now….?

Before Kaiya had a chance to knock on the large wooden door, the door swung open, the sun-shaped

149

knocker bouncing against the wood with a *thud*.

"Hello, Kaiya. Please, come in." Mr. White said, standing tall against the frame of the doorway, already leaning back into the house. A golden retriever wagged his tail behind him, poised to bark again.

She kept her head down as she crossed the threshold of the White's House. Every step was a trespass, every breath a robbery of oxygen that she was forbidden to take. Mr. White floated over the light wooden floors, the golden retriever scampering behind him. The dog would glance back at Kaiya every so often, to check that she was following? Kaiya didn't know.

She followed Mr. White through the entry room, past the living room, and into the kitchen. Everything seemed darker than she had remembered. The windows that faced the driveway had the blinds drawn, the door to Mr. White's office was closed shut. Light only streamed in through the wall of windows that looked out to Mrs. White's garden in the back of the house. If those curtains were drawn, the whole house would have been enveloped in darkness.

The silence was the worst part to deal with. Kaiya longed to say something, anything. An apology, a confession, a requiem… anything to break the stillness of the empty house.

Mr. White approached the glass door that led out to the garden, the only noise being the golden retriever's nails scraping against the hardwood. He turned the handle rather roughly and swung the door open. A rush of warm air streamed into the house, the sun beckoning the two outside. Mr. White swung his arm out, gesturing for Kaiya to go first as he held the door.

He avoided Kaiya's eyes.

Kaiya could see a figure hunched over some flower beds through the doorway but dropped her head down to watch the hardwood turn into a grassy path as she crossed the threshold into the garden.

Mrs. White looked up from her flowers at the sound of the door closing behind her husband. A shadow seemed to flash across her face when their eyes met, only to be quickly replaced with a soft smile. Mrs. White's eyes gleamed, welling up with shallow tears.

"Kaiya, it's been so long," Mrs. Abbott sighed, setting down her spade and leaning her head to the side. Though she tried to speak, the words wouldn't roll off of Kaiya's tongue.

"Come on, let's sit," Mrs. Abbott suggested. She stood up and ambled over to a trio of lawn chairs underneath a pergola adjacent to the garden. Mr. White followed first, with Kaiya trailing behind him. Once they had all sat down, the words tumbled in an avalanche.

"I'm so sorry, Mr. and Mrs. White," Kaiya sped out, her words blurring together, "I never meant to put Opal in any danger or, god-forbid, *hurt* her. I meant to come back to see you both, I really did. I was just so scared—" Kaiya paused to take a deep breath when Mrs. White grabbed her forearm.

"Kaiya, it's alright, please," Mrs. Abbott blurted, her steely blue eyes piercing into Kaiya's.

Opal had her mother's eyes.

Kaiya sucked in a deep breath, then slowly released it, her eyes never leaving Mrs. White's.

"There's nothing to be sorry for, Kaiya," Mr. White interjected, his head tilted down toward the ground. "We know that you loved Opal just as much as we did."

Mrs. White let go of Kaiya's arm. She used her now-free hand to push her blonde hair, now streaked with grey, behind her shoulder. Kaiya could see Mrs. White's face more clearly now, the lines of age beginning to etch into her sharp cheekbones. She reached out toward her husband, taking his hand in hers.

"You're not…?" Kaiya paused, trying to find the words she needed to say. "You're not angry with me? You have every right to be. I just—"

"Of course we're not angry. If anything," Mrs. White interrupted, looking up at her husband, "We're disappointed you hadn't come to us sooner."

Kaiya sucked in a breath and hiccuped. She reached up to touch her face, her cheeks damp from the tears she hadn't even realized she had shed.

"I-"

"You don't have to explain, dear," Mr. White sighed, "We all process grief in our own ways." He looked up, for the first time since he opened the front door, and his gaze fell upon Earth's satellite as she rose above the horizon. His eyes were puffy and red, strands of his greying hair plastered to his cheekbones from his tears.

No one spoke for a while after that. A family of wrens, nestled in between the branches of one of Mrs. White's apple trees, provided a chirping song to combat the growing wall of silence. The sun had started its descent beyond the Ash trees of the western horizon, streaks of pink and orange painting the sky. From across the garden, the scent of sweet, saccharine honeysuckles drifted through the humid summer air.

The honeysuckles…

Kaiya shifted in her seat, gently pulling out the golden case from her back pocket. She used the corner of her tee-shirt to smooth out the smudges on the glass face, inspecting the fragile blossom.

"What's that?" Mr. White asked, finally looking in Kaiya's direction. His eyes were glued on the case, a sort of vague recognition etched into his features.

"When I woke up in the hospital after…that night," Kaiya hesitated, her eyes jumping between Opal's parents and the flower. "The only thing I had left from Opal was this flower. So, I pressed it into one of my mother's old photo frames to keep it safe. I never quite figured out what exactly it was, though."

Mr. and Mrs. White looked at each other, a mixture of curiosity and confusion lining the glances.

"Do you mind if I…?" Mrs. White hesitantly reached out toward the case, her palm facing the sky.

Kaiya glanced back down at the case. Surely she wouldn't do anything to harm it?

But what if she knows what kind of flower it is?

"Sure," Kaiya replied, gently placing the gold-bound glass panes into Mrs. White's palm. Her eyes never left the flower as Mrs. White carefully lifted the glass up to her eyes.

After some close inspection with Mr. White leaning on his wife's shoulder, Mrs. White handed the gold frame back to Kaiya.

"Do you know what it is?" Kaiya pleaded, her eyes

shining up at her friend's mom.

"Even though it's been dried out for many years," Mrs. Abbott started, "I can say with almost full certainty that the flower you have there is a *Convolvulus arvensis*, otherwise known as Feild Bindweed or Morning Glories. They're an invasive species in Maine, so I haven't done much more research into them."

"I have, though," Mr. White interjected. He breathed in as if to continue but hesitated.

"What is it?" Kaiya asked, unconsciously leaning forward, on the edge of her seat.

"It's," Mr. White stopped, unable to bring himself to finish the sentence.

"It's alright, sweetheart. I'm right here," Mrs. White cooed, reaching her arm around her husband. Tears were starting to form in her eyes again as if she could sense what her husband was about to say.

"Morning Glories are…" Mr. White paused and took a deep breath, closing his eyes.

"Poisonous."

Mrs. White clasped her free hand over her mouth, stifling her wails. Her husband turned into Mrs. White's shoulder, gasping for breath as he cried. Kaiya looked back down at the pressed flower in her hands. Her face reddened, and not from the tears.

It wasn't even the rising tide that… got Opal.
It was a damned flower.

"You don't think…?" Kaiya started, her eyes darting between the glass, Opal's parents, and the moon on the dimming horizon. Flaming hot tears fled from Kaiya's eyes.

Mrs. White only nodded, her mouth quivering

slightly. She turned toward her husband and met his gaze. They seemed to speak to each other with their eyes for they came to a mutual decision. In unison, they each opened one arm out, waving Kaiya in for an embrace.

Even after all these years?

Kaiya slowly rose from her lawn chair, wiping away some of the tears with the back of her hand. Her anger seemed to melt away with every staggered step over to the Whites, their arms wide open. Their eyes, one green pair and one blue, called back out to Kaiya.

Of course, Kay. Just like it was yesterday.

. ⊙☾§☽⊙ .

Night had completely fallen over the small town of Acadia, Maine. Kaiya knelt on the stone floor at the far end of the greenhouse, the uneven surface temporarily denting her skin. The window was held open by a metal lever, cool night air cascading through the opening. Kaiya's arms rested on the windowsill, the glass case held precariously in her hands.

After the revelation at the White's house, Mr. and Mrs. White had offered to drive her back home, saying it was too dark and too soon to be alone. She had gladly taken the ride, an old sense of normalcy returning as she shuffled into their backseat.

Tonight, the moon shone full across Niboiwi Bay. She was so small, so much further away than the closeness Kaiya and the rest of the world had gotten used to.

"Hey, Opal," Kaiya smiled at the satellite, noticing the familiar acne scars on her surface. "I went to see your parents today. I mean, I guess you were there too." Kaiya chuckled lightly, her eyes beginning to shine.

"We figured it out. It had to have been this Morning Glory," Kaiya muttered, looking down towards the flower in its glass cage. "I just, I thought you should know. I know you said earlier that you don't remember much of that night, and, I guess, neither do I." Kaiya let silence fill the night air, the chirping crickets, and distant crashing waves being the only noise to pierce the quiet.

"I wouldn't have made the connection if it weren't for Briar," Kaiya added, her voice just above a normal speaking level now.

"She," Kaiya paused, stifling a sniffle, "She misses you just as much as I do."

Kaiya sighed, her body longing to be transported to the subject of her gaze.

"I just, I guess," Kaiya stumbled, her sights back on the glass case, "I thought you should have this." Her fingers slipped around the latch on the side of the panes. A quick move of her fingernail unlatched the cover with a light *click*. Kaiya carefully opened the case, sliding the Morning Glory delicately onto the palm of her hand.

"I hope that you're doing alright up there, O. I just," Kaiya sighed, "I just wanted to let you know that I love you." Kaiya closed her eyes and blew the flower into the night, trusting that the ocean breeze would carry it back to Opal. A single tear trickled down Kaiya's cheek, finding a home in the corner of her lips.

She opened her eyes, and with great gentleness, Kaiya closed the now empty gold case shut. As she rose to her feet, her eyes fell upon the moon once more, her surface shining light for all to see. Kaiya turned away, trudging her way back through the greenhouse and into her house. Her *home*.

She'll never really be gone, will she?

Opal will stay with me, with everyone, for as long as the moon circles the sky.

If anything, she'll live amongst the heavens.

Until we meet again, O, on the other side of the stars.

Epilogue.

August twenty-sixth, 2025.

Kaiya Abbott closed the storefront's door, a hanging bell jingling on the handle. She deftly turned the key, the lock closing with a *click*, and returned the key to her sunflower lanyard. *The Celestial Specialty Shoppe*, her pride and joy, was situated toward the end of Downtown Acadia's main street boulevard.

As Kaiya waltzed away from her small business, she peered into its windows. The main room was dim, only a small amount of dusky sunlight streaming in through the glass panes. A row of easels faced the street, their canvas-covered wooden frames standing guard as the protectors of the shop.

Behind the easels, a few polished-off pottery wheels sat stationary before the rows of shelves. Her items ranged from clay mugs and bowls to paintings and woven art strung up on the walls. The shop was always bursting with color, its customers even livelier than the art they produced.

A vintage telephone ringing pierced the late summer air, emanating from Kaiya's back pocket. She always did love the juxtaposition of the old with the new.

Kaiya slipped her phone out of her paint-splattered jeans and slid her finger across the screen. The ringing stopped, a familiar profile picture taking up the center of the screen.

Speaking of lively.

"Hiya, Bo," Kaiya smiled to herself, gliding down main street to her usual bus stop.

"Hey, Kaiya! I just wanted to check in and see how your day was going," Briar exclaimed, her warmth practically flowing through the phone speakers.

"It was wonderful, Briar. I held a pottery spinning class this morning as well as worked on my latest tapestry. You should stop by between one of your classes to come to see it," Kaiya rambled, perfectly content with just speaking with Briar. She's been so in and out of the house lately, that it was hard to find some quality time together.

"Oh, good! I'm so glad your day went well," Briar babbled, "I just wanted to let you know that I have a surprise for you after you get home and all cleaned up."

Kaiya almost ran into the stop sign before the bus station, her mind wandering.

"Suprise?"

"Yup!" Briar cheered, "As you're probably well aware, being a mathematics and physics double major can lead to a lot of schoolwork and library hours at the university."

"You can say that again," Kaiya giggled, poking fun

at Briar's busy schedule.

"Anyways!" Briar continued gleefully, a hint of taunting in her tone. "I cleared away everything from the schedule tonight so it can be just you and me and my little surprise!"

Kaiya laughed, tilting her head back, the sky's fiery sunset colors basking the street in a rosy glow. She leaned against the bus stop, her hand cradling Briar's voice.

"Well, I'm just about to jump on the bus to get back home. Is there anything else you need while I'm out?" Kaiya asked, her mind's eye swiping through images of a lavish dinner, a puppy tied with a ribbon, and a ring.

"Just you, Kay. That's all I need," Briar said, smug and satisfied with her sly remark.

"Hey—!" Kaiya started, jolting back as the Acadia bus screeched to a halt on her left. The doors swung open with an aerated *psht*.

"Well," Briar giggled, "It looks like your ride is here."

"Yeah, yeah," Kaiya managed, still catching her breath from both Briar's remark and the bus. She shuffled her phone in the crook of her shoulder and her ear in order to get out her bus pass. "I gotta get on, now. I'll see you at home?"

"I can't wait," Briar gushed, "See you soon. I love you!"

"I love you too," Kaiya cooed, smiling as she clicked off the call.

Kaiya mounted the stairs to the bus with feet as light as a feather. With a quick flash of her bus pass, the driver waved her inside. She walked a few rows back and swung herself into a seat. The rest of the bus was relatively empty, an old ukulele song playing softly through the bus's outdated speakers.

Is that...?

Eyes closed, Kaiya strained her ears to hear the music, its distant familiarity loosening memories of a grand piano.

"Somewhere, over the rainbow,"
"Bluebirds fly."

Kaiya's lips turned up into a light smile, a warmth spreading from her heart down through her limbs. She nestled back into her seat, a largely uncomfortable carpeted bench, and pulled out the familiar gold case, smoothing the edges with her thumb and forefinger. Instead of a flower, a photograph had been placed in between the glass panes, depicting Niboiwi Bay at dusk. Briar and Kaiya stood in the sand, their arms wrapped tightly around each other. Goofy, wide grins were plastered across their cheeks, their eyes crinkled from laughter. Rising behind them, far off on the horizon, the moon stood guard over her loved ones. A picture of the perfect union between the moon, the tides, and the Earth.

You see, everyone raves about the truest love story of the sun and the moon, distant, opposites. Yet, soon shall come to pass the day where all will know the story of when the moon fell in love with the tide.

Acknoweledgments

I'd like to take a moment to thank some very special people. Without you all, this book wouldn't have been possible. First and foremost, I'd like to thank my wonderfully amazing-intelligent-spunky-cool creative writing teacher, Ms. Jessica Dyche. Her experience and guidance throughout this extensive creative process have been completely invaluable. On days when I felt stuck or like giving up, her comments always reinstated my confidence in myself. Ms. Dyche, I cannot thank you enough for how you've changed me as a writer. Cheers to earning your doctorate!

Next, I'd like to thank Betty Phan and Lyric Blevins, my two absolutely wonderful editors and some of my closest friends. We did it! We made it through a tough year together, and I couldn't have asked for anyone better to be in our supernatural-mystery-Sapphic-fiction novella group! Without your ideas, comfort, and guidance, When the Moon Fell wouldn't be the book it is today. So, thank you!

Of course, some major thanks are in order to my AWESOME family. Dad, thank you for helping me think through my writer's block and remain confident in my own abilities as a writer. Without you, I might have given up on this story altogether. Mom, thank you for being so gentle with me. You always asked if there was anything I needed, anything you could help with to take some stress off of my shoulders. You cut me some slack on those late nights, and I couldn't have finished this book without your encouragement.

To my younger siblings, thank you for your patience. I know that I can be a ticking-time bomb when I'm stressed, and, for the most part, you two handled it with grace. Ashley, I appreciate those nights that you would bring down a glass of water to my bedroom, reminding me to take a break. Whenever I was in need of a hug, you were right by my side. Your timing is impeccable, hon. Mads, thank you for bearing with me through this process. You put up with my angry morning tirades on the way to school and you'd scream out music in the car on our way to get coffee, which was my main fuel for this project. I also can't forget that your incredible skills made this cover! Sure, I may seem frustrated with you because you're good at everything first try, but seriously, your art really tied this project together for me.

I'm one of the luckiest people imaginable because I've been gifted a found family that lightens my life. To Déja Clarke, a toast to all of our book-store dates and talking endlessly about fantasy worlds. Thank you for keeping up with the whole writing process, it means the world to me.

To Meghan Haldeman, my day one. Thank you for being there for me and going on spontaneous shopping sprees with me. You were a huge help in keeping me motivated, and I couldn't ever thank you enough. I'm also pretty sure that both you and Déja finished this book in one sitting, but that's alright with me.

To Zia Francis and Brielle Kemavor, thank you for being the best hype girls a girl could ask for. Your energy and enthusiasm, even if reading isn't really your thing, have been absolutely paramount in this journey. Thank you for sharing your light. <3

During the very final stretch of the creation of this novel, the wonderfully amazing Maia Ward helped me IMMENSELY with my chapter dividers and other Macbook related wizardry. I love you, bestie!

To room 1313 and all of the party people within, thank you for providing a space that fostered my creative abilities.

Lastly, I would like to thank you, the reader. You didn't have to grab this book, read it, or even open it. But, you did. All I've ever wanted was to tell stories that mean something to someone. I hope that someone is you.

Thank you. <3

~MJB

Somewhere over the rainbow...
Bluebirds fly.

~ Israel Kamakawiwo'ole

Makayla Bowman is a graduate of the Center for Fine and Performing Arts Creative Writing program at Colgan High School. She will attend the University of Mary Washington as a member of their Honor's College, varsity volleyball team, and class of 2026. When she's not writing, Makayla spends her time surrounded by nature and the ones she loves. Her other works of short fiction and poetry have been published by Off the Wall, Siren, and The Megalodon literary magazines.

<3

CPSIA information can be obtained
at www.ICGtesting.com
Printed in the USA
LVHW090251130522
718352LV00002BA/139